Lita

ALSO BY JERVEY TERVALON

Living for the City

Understand This

Dead Above Ground

All the Trouble You Need

Lita

a novel

JERVEY TERVALON

WSP

New York London Toronto Sydney

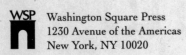 Washington Square Press
1230 Avenue of the Americas
New York, NY 10020

ISBN: 0-7434-4884-7
        0-7434-4885-5 (Pbk)

First Washington Square Press trade paperback edition May 2004

10 9 8 7 6 5 4 3 2 1

For information regarding special discounts for bulk purchases, please contact Simon & Schuster Special Sales at 1-800-456-6798 or business@simonandschuster.com

Manufactured in the United States of America

For Lita

Acknowledgments

With the generous help of family and friends this novel was made possible. Gina, my lovely and compelling wife's patience and indulgence is deeply appreciated, as is my wonderful daughter Giselle's interest in various plot points and details. Elise, our ever-engaging baby girl, is carrying around books and stacking them high, manifesting a fine appreciation of the written word. Now, if only my nieces, Amber, Mononique, and Terencia, and nephew, Shanon, would open a book of mine! Thanks to my cousin Ellen Hazeur for the generous contribution of a passage or so on page 43. I expect her first novel to be gracing bookstores soon enough. And to my family in New Orleans for being such a template to hang fiction upon.

I'd also like to thank the California Arts Council for the fiction fellowship I received; and the Adalia Book Club: Katherine L. Coleman, Lisa Franklin, Alycia Gardner Moore, Esq., Darecia Scott, Connie Sulker-Hall,

Acknowledgments

Pamela A. Taylor, and Terri Williams for the invitation to dine and discuss *Dead Above Ground*. The red beans were delicious! Thanks to Pitzer College for the writing residency; Occidental College, and the Center for African-American Studies at UCLA, for those institutions' continued support.

And I need to say a farewell to our dog, Hersey, who decided to return to Alaska and his ancestors. May he forever frolic in fresh snow.

And lastly, much love to my mother, Lolita Villavaso Tervalon, for her faith in me, her gumbo, and most importantly for not suing the hell out of me.

"Life is real, life is earnest, and because (with apologies to Longfellow) the grave is unambiguously its end if not its goal some of the loveliest and best of us, Criseyde for example, can't resist the choice of lingering awhile among even its lesser pleasures; life is full of choices, not necessarily right versus wrong; life is plural and defines itself against life; life is too emphatic to get lost in the words on a page."

—Marvin Mudrick, from the preface of *Nobody Here but Us Chickens*

Lita

Part One

1

The phone rang at 4:00 A.M. with news that Daddy was on his deathbed and I needed to come home to New Orleans. Confused, I took a minute or two to get my head clear, then I panicked. Suddenly, I was a little girl about to lose her father, sinking below despair, but that despair vanished when I got my wits about me.

It was Daddy she was talking about.

I had detested him all my life. Why should I pretend to care about him on his deathbed? Waste of time and money to go to New Orleans, rushing home to say last words. I had no last words for him, this man who never did a thing for us—except to beat Mother when he felt like it.

I was surprised that it took me a moment to recognize that voice I hadn't heard in more than ten years.

Made me want to laugh, Aunt Dot trying to sound like a sane person.

"Lita, you need to come back. You've been gone too long," she said.

I shook my head.

"No disrespect, Aunt Dot, but I don't think I've been gone long enough."

"Lita, that's all water under the bridge."

"Guess it is," I said, with so little enthusiasm even a lunatic like her should have picked up on it.

"How are the kids?" Aunt Dot asked, as though she cared.

"Just fine. Everybody is about as fine as they can be."

She hummed a bit, as if she wanted to say something, but couldn't bring herself to get to it. I imagined it was a bit of poison that she had been carrying around for the last decade, waiting for that right moment to slip it to me. That's what I expected from a woman who sicced her crazy boys on me, scratched my face bloody the day before my wedding over forty dollars she said I owed her.

"I saw her," Aunt Dot said, like I should know what she's talking about.

"Saw who?" I asked tentatively, regretting the question as soon as I asked it.

"At the house on Gravier. I saw her in the bedroom."

Too tired to play Aunt Dot's guessing game, I wanted to be done with the conversation. I should have hung up—I had every right to hang up on Aunt Dot—but I was fool enough to listen, now I was fouled up in her line.

"Helen."

"Mother? What are you saying? You saw Mother?"

"Yeah, I did. Other people saw her too, your sisters, not just me."

"Stop joking. I don't have time for this."

"Lita, it's a sign, a sign for you to come home."

I slammed the phone down so hard it sounded like a gunshot in that sleeping house.

I had a clue of what was going on down there; I had an inheritance coming. Once Daddy's dead we're to sell Mother's house and divide the proceeds. I got Mother's will and I read it, and unlike Aunt Dot, I understand it. If I don't agree to sell, Aunt Dot won't get her cut, and even though I could use the money, I don't want to sell.

Aunt Dot calling with crazy nonsense might have jarred me awake and wasted my time, but I almost welcomed the distraction. The way things have been going in Los Angeles, getting stirred up about New Orleans is almost a relief.

L.A. isn't the promised land I thought it would be when we first arrived, and certainly not now. I don't know what I could have been thinking—streets paved with gold, platinum toilets — that kind of nonsense. Los Angeles is just another city, brutal and cruel, but with palm trees and freeways and dreams of a better life.

Ten years ago we arrived and moved into Winston's cousin's house on Second Avenue that we bought from him sight unseen, and the lousy bastard had the lights and heat turned off on us, I guess to save a couple of dollars and get his deposit back a couple of days sooner.

We rolled in after three days of hellish driving across hot miles and miles of Texas, New Mexico, and Arizona deserts. I was six months pregnant, trying not to throw up out the window, doing my best to keep the kids from driving me nuts, but I was already nuts from that husband of mine whistling every song he learned in three years of army life.

I have no words to describe how happy I was to get to Los Angeles, even if the sky was brown and the air burned my eyes. I was out of that stupid car after days of being packed in like funky sardines.

That first night we ate ham and cheese po'boys by candlelight. That was nice, but I have good ears and I could hear skittering in the plaster walls of this house that I expected to be some kind of wonderful.

"Your goddamn brother's house has rats!" I whispered to Winston, so I wouldn't wake the children. "You better get rid of them tomorrow or I'm turning around and going back to New Orleans."

He looked at me like I had lost my mind.

"Lita, I don't hear no rats."

Lita

"Then you're deaf," I said, and turned over and
went to sleep.

Winston missed sounds and words you'd think he'd
catch, having damaged one ear in the war; he always
managed, though, to hear what you didn't expect him
to, specially whispers under my breath about how he
was making me crazy enough to kill him.

7

The next morning the air was crisp, the smog had
blown off, and we could see mountains in the distance.
I even saw the Hollywood sign for the first time. It was
a plain beautiful day, crisp and sharp with seagulls flying in the blue sky. The neighborhood was clean and
the neighbors friendly; the streets broad, the houses
Craftsman, not shotgun. I thought I could be happy.
Winston certainly was happy with the big garage he
could work on cars in. The children ran wild in the big
yard with lemon and peach trees to climb and thick St.
Augustine grass to roll on. For a time I was pleased
with our decision to move to Los Angeles. I forgot all
about that first night: lack of heat and lights, and even
those rats in the walls of my little dream home.

Ava and Ana didn't seem nervous about their new
school, the Holy Name of Jesus Christ, but after

watching Sister Patrell escort the girls to their desks, it was obvious that this brown-skinned Oriental woman didn't care for them. They sat next to each other, twin bookends in their black-and-white-plaid school uniforms with their tightly braided and oiled hair, and their hands crossed like attentive angels. It didn't matter that the teacher didn't like them. They did fine in school, and nothing Sister Patrell could do or say touched them. They were beautiful, and I was proud to be their big sister.

I had no idea that my little sisters were plotting to escape; they were sick of me and of my heavy-handed ways.

Richie, too, would be heading back to Louisiana as soon as he could figure out how. Richie, my young cousin that Mother took in, was like a dog that had been beaten once too many times; something was wrong in his head. Even if he wanted to do right, it wouldn't happen. I asked him to go up in the attic to take out a rat Winston had poisoned. Usually Winston would get them down, but he was off chasing down parts for a transmission, and I couldn't stand the reek wafting from the ceiling. Richie scrambled up the ladder and found that rat in no time. The boy was more excited than he had a right to be. The next few days he continued sneaking up into the attic, looking for more poisoned rats. I guess I should have been happy that the boy wanted to help out, but something about him all juiced up to crawl around in the blackness searching for rotting rats unnerved me. I told him not to go back up into the attic, that he had no business up there.

He gave me such a sullen, disrespectful sneer that I slapped him down. I wasn't Mother, but he had to respect and listen to me.

He wouldn't go to school unless I threatened to beat him, but that didn't work. Because of Aunt Dot he knew how to take a whipping, and wasn't afraid of them. I'd wear my arm down beating his butt, and it wouldn't change a thing. I didn't have to worry about his attendance for very long because he spit on a nun and got thrown out of Holy Name. I put him in a public school, but soon the truant officer called, trying to find him. Richie stopped going after his first day.

Winston tried talking to Richie, and of course that was a big mistake because he ended up yelling at him. Richie ran away. A neighbor found him sleeping in a doghouse with the man's hunting dogs. We brought him home and got him clean, but a few days later he took off again. He spent the night at the bowling alley on Crenshaw, then the next night it was beneath the trees at Rancho Park. Then he found his way to the Greyhound depot miles away. Each time we found him, I whipped his behind, but it didn't matter. Quick enough, he was gone again, vanishing into the night.

He was practicing to leave us for good.

I don't know how far Richie thought he'd get with no money—to New Orleans? Even if he did, I hoped he didn't believe that Aunt Dot would take him back.

9

She had to be the meanest bitch of a mother who ever lived. I'd bet my last dollar that if he could manage to find his way to New Orleans, Dot would kick him off the porch like he was the mangiest cur that ever wandered up the steps.

If anybody would be able to take care of himself, it would be Richie. He was big for thirteen and the kind of kid who would have gotten a job in New Orleans on the docks in the old days.

He missed Mother more than any of us, and his want for her just got worse. Being around us was just another reminder of his loss.

I understood.

Though Mother died years ago, it still felt like a fresh wound. The twins grew up with that too, as though at any moment Mother would come through the door, puffing from that bad heart of hers, struggling with a pot roast or some such thing she'd be planning on cooking for Daddy's dinner.

Wasn't a thing I could do for Richie but not get too furious when I discovered that he had slipped fifty dollars from my purse.

I got word that he did make it back to New Orleans, and found a bed with the Sisters of Mercy. I wondered how long it would be before he'd sneak out of the orphanage on his way to somewhere else.

2

*After a year or so, we more or less accli-*mated to Los Angeles. It wasn't us against this strange new world any longer, forcing us to bind together to make it through the day. No, everyone had their own agendas, specially the twins. They had something going on, something behind those whispers, little gestures, hands concealing strips of paper with scribbled codes. With them I was always on the outside, overhearing bits and shards of their private language.

What were they plotting?

What pissed me off about them was that they really didn't need me. If I drove them out to Death Valley and tossed them out, no doubt they'd make it back with cool drinks in hand. Now they were no longer pretty little matching bookends, resigned to doing what I said.

Mother taught me, though I hated her heavy hand, you had to get respect, even if you had to beat somebody's behind. Those girls, even when they were doing whatever chores I gave them, defied me with their sullen looks and cutting glances. Mother wouldn't have put up with it. She would have slapped them silly first, and asked questions later. I didn't want to resort to Mother's tactics, but often I couldn't help myself. I would get mad, and then I would just explode. It was easy, too easy to fall into.

The twins thought of themselves as grown at twelve.

Now almost four years later they were ready to put me in my place. It was three women under one roof; two against one. No matter how I tried to get them to realize they weren't grown, they persisted. Of course they kept silent, still frightened that I would slap them down if they got in my face. They were right, I would and did. I wanted to be done with raising them. If only there was some magic I could do to make time speed up and get the twins on their way.

What had I done to find myself in this family? I went to church; I lit candles, observed Lent, ate fish on Friday. Hell of a lot of good that did me.

This new trouble, I should have seen it coming like a fat, flying cockroach.

Overnight Ava became a woman.

I looked up from the dinner table to ask Ava to pass the ham, and I saw it for the first time. Though, I don't know how I could have missed it. Ava and Ana no longer were mirror images; one of them had become a brick house.

Ava was now a Creole Lana Turner, with a bosom that sprouted overnight like wicked mushrooms.

Ana, on the other hand, still was flat, still looked like a girl, and she wasn't happy about it.

Winston noticed, and he looked intimidated. He tried his best to ignore Ava's new cleavage by adjusting his chair so that he faced the wall and not the rest of us at the dining table. Much as he wanted to, he couldn't help glancing at her, and that man practiced restraint like it was a commandment.

I sent Ava to bed before she finished pecking at her dinner. Soon as she left, I could breathe, like somehow air had rushed back into the room.

*A*va, *defiantly proud* of her new endowments, preened about the house like she had invented the whole idea of breasts.

They were a wonder, those things. The girl's seventeenth birthday wasn't for a couple of months, and already she was bigger than me. I shook my head, knowing what kind of trouble those mounds of flesh were going to cause.

That was the last day that Ana would sit next to Ava at the dinner table or at school. A wall sprang up between them, and it was as surprising as it was sad.

13

They were closer to each other than any other human being on earth, and now they were as separate as siblings could be. No longer did they wear the same hairstyle and outfits; they didn't talk to each other with that conspiratorial intensity that they had been sharing their whole lives.

They were trying to be as different as they could manage; or maybe it was just Ana, trying to put miles between herself and the relationship that had defined her. Ava was too busy being spellbound by her spanking new breasts even to notice how shell-shocked Ana had become. Stopping and staring at any surface that would reflect her new dimensions, she didn't have a spare minute. Those things had power over me too; I began treating Ava differently. What I used to get mad at, I silently accepted, but only from Ava. Ana continued to come to the dinner table; Ava stayed in the bedroom like she had better things to do than eat with the family. I put up with it. That was her choice. Moviestar cleavage clouded my judgment. All you needed to be a woman was a pair of knockers; forget all about needing the constitution of a horse, the patience of Job, and a back that won't break.

Again at the sewing machine, working hard to let out Ava's blouses and jackets, I wanted her to know how hard this was on everybody but her. Seemed all that mattered for Ava was that the cotton strained against the three top buttons of her blouse, threatening to burst open and reveal her cleavage to the world. I stopped sewing and waved her over to me.

"Listen, Ava, you're not a girl anymore. You've got to be careful."

I had already let her school uniform jacket out as far as it could go; there wasn't enough material to gain a quarter inch. Resigned to sewing a new school uniform so she wouldn't look like a sausage about to pop out of its casing, I got out my measuring tape.

She shrugged, as though she didn't have any interest in what I was talking about.

"Are you listening to me?"

I got her up on a chair and took measurements; Lord, she was 36C easily.

Ava laughed.

"What the hell are you laughing at, Ava?"

"I'm careful," she said, still giggling, looking away from me.

Ana, who was at the dining room table doing her homework, chortled loudly.

"What's going on with her?" I asked Ana.

"A lot! Ask her."

"Shut up, Ana!" Ava said.

"You shut up," I said, smacking her on the side of the head. "I'm the only one here who gets to tell anybody to shut up."

I turned back to Ana.

"So what does she know?"

Ana lit up, like giving me the lowdown on Ava was something she was going to enjoy.

"She talks to men on the way home. Sometimes the men get out of their cars, and she stops to listen to what they got to say."

I took a deep breath. I didn't want to start strangling Ava, not yet.

"You're not talking to men on the way home, are you?"

"Sometimes," she said.

Rage, red and more red! I shot up and slapped Ava from the chair, and she tumbled backward on her ass, her legs way above her head. As good as it felt to hit her, I felt contempt for myself, as deep as that river that followed me out west.

Ava looked up at me, terror in her eyes.

"Don't you ever so long as you live talk to strange men. I don't give a damn how big your tits are!"

Then I was out of the house, rushing into the cold, dry air of a December night.

I walked awhile, circling the block, and kept going until I reached the liquor store, scowled at the men by the telephone booth whistling at me, headed in and looked at the pickled pig feet in the big green jar on the counter, decided against buying one, and walked back to the house.

I sat on the porch, hating my temper. It was getting worse, anger exploding out of me, but I'd be lying if I said it didn't feel good to give in to it. I was getting to be more like Mother with each passing day, just as incapable of stopping my fists from flying when things weren't right.

I wanted to go into the house and apologize to Ava, to explain to her why I got so mad. She was too young to understand all that went on with Adele and Lucien, and why even her looking in a man's direction would make my heart beat like a bass drum. Thinking of Adele made me feel sick to my stomach, how beautiful she was, how she lived too hard and stupidly. I never in a million years will understand why she decided to do what she did, give herself to a man who had killed women and got away with it. Did she do it just because he was beautiful? I was there on the porch that day Mother explained to Adele what kind of man Lucien was, and Adele shook her head and laughed. Told Mother she didn't know Lucien, that he was sweet as could be. I think all Mother succeeded in doing was making Adele run as fast as she could into the arms of Lucien. Once he had her, that bastard turned her out, broke her down, and did his best to keep her down. Then when she got the strength to leave him, he killed her, tossed her into a trunk, and threw her into the Mississippi. Mother found out all she could about what happened between Lucien and Adele. More than likely she was still alive when he put her in that trunk. Did that rat bastard know that Adele was pregnant for him?

He wouldn't have cared. Yeah, he was some kind of monster.

*A*va *was still* a girl, everything was new and shiny to her, and nobody could tell her a thing, just like Adele. You'd think a man might notice that, but that's why men make me sick to my stomach. Sure, she had a woman's shape, but even an idiot could see that she had the face of a child. Nature plays games and makes girls women before they have the chance to understand what kind of a mess they can make of their lives. Anybody should see that she's a girl, but no, some fool with a thing between his legs chases her down walking home from school. God, if I saw that I would have run back for Winston's shotgun. One thing I've learned, and I've learned this lesson well, you've got to protect yourself and what's yours. If a sweet-faced snake slides up with honey-laced lies, you need to cut its head off.

Don't play, just kill it.

Life is some kind of war, and every battle just leads to another battle that's more important than the last one, and you can't lose any of them, because losing is Adele floating in a trunk in the Mississippi.

I don't need to be loved.

It doesn't matter if the girls love me. After all I've seen, I'd rather they grow up fearing me and not being a fool for some man to come along and love them to death.

How can a woman ignore what's right in front of her, and damn sure walk a path to the graveyard? What did Mother call it, "graveyard love"?

19

*W*hen *I finally* did decide to return to the house, the girls scattered like rabbits, scared of what I might do. I sighed as I sat down on the sofa and turned off the lights. I had no idea what I was capable of, and like the girls, I didn't want to find out.

ig Winston came into the house angry as a bee, but I could tell that he was unnerved, even scared, and that red-faced anger was mostly bluff. I had seen that look enough in New Orleans, when everything was going bad with Adele.

"Your Aunt Odie is on the porch," he said softly, like the devil was knocking to get in.

"Why is she on the porch? Let her into the house!"

Winston shook his head and returned to the door. He didn't like to be talked to sharply, but sometimes he didn't think.

Aunt Odie came in walking as erect as a flagpole at, what? She had to be seventy-five, at least. She looked like a shadow dressed in white, walking into three o'clock sun. Her face was even more skeletal and

severe, but once she stepped past Winston, she smiled
warmly at the twins and my two playing at my feet.
She hugged me, and I could feel all the bones in her
rail-thin back.

"Aunt Odie, I didn't know you were in Los Angeles."

I offered her a chair. After glaring at Big Winston
until he retreated from the house into the backyard, she
sat down.

"I'm here on business for my church."

I nodded, wondering what kind of business a
church of voodoo worshipers would have in Los Angeles. Maybe looking for gilded splinters to buy?

"I got a message that you needed help."

"From whom?" I asked.

Aunt Odie didn't bother to answer.

The twins came into the room and sat on the couch
next to each other for the first time in recent memory.

I looked at them, and I knew that they had called
Aunt Odie behind my back. I guess they needed rescuing from me as much as I needed rescuing from
them.

"Do you two want to go with Aunt Odie? Just say
so. I won't stand in your way."

I was sure Ava was going to hop up, waving her
hand, ready to sprout wings and fly anywhere I wasn't.
She couldn't have me out of her sight fast enough.
Don't know what she was thinking, though; Aunt Odie
was razor-strap stricter than me. Hell, she was stricter
than Mother.

"Are you going to stay with us a few days?" I asked.

"No, child, I've got to get back to Louisiana. Ana, go pack your things!"

"Ana?" I said.

Ana looked away from me as she hurried to the bedroom.

Ava smiled broadly as though she knew she had caught me flatfooted. I wanted her to go with Aunt Odie; Odie would know what to do, how to raise that child.

"Aunt Odie, you mean you don't plan to take Ava? I don't think those two could stand to be parted."

Aunt Odie sighed and waved for Ava to come over. She took her time about crossing that short distance, and I felt like whacking her on the behind. Aunt Odie reached for Ava's hand and turned her about, appraising her sprung voluptuousness.

I never heard Aunt Odie whistle before, but she did, high and sharp like she was commenting on a fastball. Shaking her head in amazement at Ava's blossomed womanhood, she summed up her feelings in a weary voice.

"Lita, I'm an old woman. I'm prepared to do what I can for Helen's children, but I don't have the energy to fend off the wolves that are going to be at the door of this one."

Ava smiled like the fattest and sassiest Cheshire cat,

exulting in the fact that it would be me stuck with defending her round behind.

"What about a boarding school?" I asked, desperate for a solution.

"Now, Lita, you can't foster off your problems, the family's problems."

"Aunt Odie, you see what I'm up against." I guess the dejection showed in my voice. Aunt Odie patted my hand, then squeezed it hard. She knew exactly what I'd be up against. She turned to Ava and grabbed her pretty chin with her long, steely fingers.

"Listen, child, your sister is trying to do right by you. You got to listen to her because she knows what you have to learn, that the world is a harsh teacher, and sometimes you get no second lesson."

Aunt Odie looked into Ava's eyes, and saw what I had been seeing since her condition started, defiance as broad as the ocean.

Aunt Odie grabbed her ear and gave it a twist.

"Where is your mind?"

Ava shrugged. Maybe she had no idea where it had flown to; a world of dime-store romances?

Slowly Ava's eyes seemed to clear, and she sighed and shrugged.

"What?" she asked, like we had just appeared and pulled her down to earth with our annoying questions.

"What were you thinking about?" Aunt Odie asked.

"Nothing," Ava replied, her eyes already starting to gloss over with distraction.

"Don't lie," I said.

Aunt Odie gestured for me to be quiet, then she whispered something to Ava.

Ava looked alarmed. Aunt Odie must have threatened to cut her hair off, or something worse.

"I'm not thinking about nothing: clothes, boys."

"Boys!" I repeated. It was hopeless.

"You are too young to be thinking about boys!"

Ava turned to me and smirked.

"Why?" she asked, our eyes met. "Girls think about boys."

"Not in our family."

Ava rolled her eyes.

My hand shot out and slapped her face.

After Adele, even a child should know that answer.

*A*unt *Odie got* Ana out the door, and I was left with the powder keg that was Ava. I sighed and pulled myself together. I realized I had been ignoring my own kids. Little Winnie was pulling at my dress for dinner, and Jude was crying himself to sleep in my lap.

Ava returned to the bedroom, which was now hers alone.

I wondered what she thought of. Maybe she didn't

think, maybe it was one long sensation that girl felt; hands running along her body, passions that took her breath away, explosions that shook all of her.

It made me want to beat her behind. Rush in and toss a bucket of cold water on her imagination, as if that would do anything but steam up the mirrors.

I didn't trust any of it, getting drunk on passion. I guess I was born that way.

25

With a man like Daddy standing like a beacon, warning me about what love can get you. Yeah, and then there's Lucien. It's so easy to see—if a woman is weak, you get taken advantage of—maybe a brutal beating to boot, that's Daddy. Or, in Lucien's case, you just get dead.

I knocked at Ava's door and pushed it open. There she was on the bed, sitting cross-legged, in a cotton nightgown, brushing her hair, so absorbed she didn't notice me and probably wouldn't have noticed if Dracula had been flapping outside her window.

"Ava," I said.

She looked up.

"We need to work on a few things. Get them out in the open, here and now."

She looked at me without any fear, more confident in the days since Aunt Odie left.

"Lita, I'm not the child you think I am."

I shook my head, wondering if I should even respond.

"You think you know everything. You think you

were the only one who saw those things with Adele and Mother, but there's a lot that you don't know."

"Please, Ava, you don't know what the hell you're talking about. What could you possibly know? And what the hell difference would it make? I'm supposed to treat you like a grown-up and do what you want?"

"No, but you ought to respect me. You're not my mother; you're my sister."

"Your sassy ass is under my roof, and till you move out, what I say goes."

I stood and turned my back to her, ready to go about my business. I needed to reclaim my authority with her, but it was as much a bluff as anything.

"There's a lot you don't know," she said.

"Like what? I know you're driving me crazy."

"You don't know all of it."

"All of what?" I asked, taking a half step in her direction.

"What happened to us when you were off being married. You always got something to say about how we got to do this and that. You've been doing that for years now, so now you got to listen to me for once in your life."

"I don't have time for this. I don't have time to care about anything else but what's in the here and now."

That's when I left her there to start dinner. I didn't need to hear that crap, some stupid attempt at making me feel guilty.

Then Ava followed me into the kitchen.

"Listen, Lita," she said.

We both sat at the kitchen table, but I couldn't help shaking my head. I didn't have time to waste on this girl. I had already wasted enough for a lifetime. She started in on telling her little story with anger in her eyes. A story I didn't want to hear, trapped in a hot kitchen, compelled to listen.

4

Ava

With Mother gone and the house half burned down, we had to go with you while Daddy rebuilt. Now, in your mind you were supposed to be Mother, but Mother was dead and you could never be Mother no matter how much you tried.

We let you talk because that's what you do, talk. You don't listen to anybody. That's why we stopped talking to you unless you made us. You didn't see what was there, right in front of you. You didn't know nothing about it, but when Richie got back from the hospital, his face and hands bandaged up from the fire that Lucien started to kill Mother, Richie couldn't stop crying. Sadder than we were about Mother, not crying 'cause of his burns, but because of how much he loved her. Me and Ana talked to him harder than we had ever talked to anybody to get him to calm down, 'cause right then and there, I thought he *would kill himself or somebody. You never could talk to Richie, so he never told you what happened that night Mother died. He didn't feel he owed you that. She loved him, and he knew you didn't. He was just a burden to you. Richie might have been crazy, but he knew you wanted him gone. Now you got your way, not really trying to stop Richie from leaving. Long time ago Ana said you wanted him to go back to Aunt Dot, but you knew that Mother didn't want that.*

You couldn't get rid of us. You were stuck with us, but how do you think we felt being stuck with you?

Richie knew you wanted him gone, so he started sleeping outside, underneath the back stairs. You told him to stop doing that too, but it didn't work. I missed Mother every day, and me and Ana cried ourselves to sleep thinking about her, but Richie was going crazy with grief.

Then we heard that Lucien was still alive, but burned up like a piece of charcoal.

We heard you talking about him to Aunt Odie.

"Darlene from Xavier works the burn ward. I told her about Lucien, and she said she'd take care of it. Murderers get special treatment. The only painkiller he'll get is after they bury him. You come near Charity Hospital, and you can hear him scream from the fourth-floor burn ward down to the street."

It was funny how you talked in front of us like we weren't even there, like we couldn't understand English. Then when you saw us looking, six eyes on you, you got upset. So what, we thought. Without saying a word, we knew we had to do something. We all needed to see Lucien before he died; see him suffering for what he did to Mother, to Adele.

Ana came up with a plan, and it was a good one. We were going to pay Lucien a visit. At first we weren't going to tell Richie, but I convinced Ana that we should. We owed him that. We sneaked out when you were sleeping with baby Winnie. We walked and walked to that hospital. Richie said he knew where it was, that we could get there in a short time, but our outfits,

sailor dresses Mother had bought for us, were soaked with sweat and we still weren't close. Richie was so far ahead I was worried we'd lose sight of him and get lost and we'd never make it to the hospital, but he looked so much like a ragpicker in his overalls, we didn't really want to walk with him.

"Where is that hospital?" Ana asked. "I'm so tired of walking."

"I don't know. I thought you knew."

We both were good and lost. Only way we were getting to the hospital was to keep up with Richie. Ana started running, and I was right behind her. We kept going until I couldn't catch my breath.

Richie stood at the corner of a ugly building, looking up like he expected someone to come falling down.

"That's the hospital," Richie said.

"I don't hear no man screaming," I said.

"We oughta go in," Richie said.

"How we gonna do that?" I asked. "I don't know nothing about hospitals."

Richie shrugged and headed into the hospital. He waved for us to follow, but I didn't know If I wanted to. Ana was just as scared as me.

"I don't know the way home," she said.

Neither did I.

We both tore after Richie.

Inside, the hospital smelled of a bathtub of witch hazel or bleach, good thing they had so many fans going on otherwise I think I would have gagged. We saw Richie talking to a nurse sitting at a desk.

"Boy, you go sit in the colored section," I heard her say.

"Ma'am, I'm just asking where they got them burned people?" Richie said.

He was doing his best to be nice, but Richie really ain't like that. He's alright most of the time to us and lets us have our way and all, but if you ain't family, he'd just as soon as kick your guts out like he does cats. Don't let him see no cats, yeah.

"They don't want to talk to him 'cause he's colored," Ana said.

We both started looking around for somebody colored we could talk to.

Ana pointed to a brown-skinned lady in white.

They both looked at me like it was my job to talk to her.

She noticed me looking at her and smiled at me.

"You lost, little girl?"

I shook my head.

"I can't find my Daddy. I think he's in that burned people ward."

The nurse looked sad for me.

"Your Daddy's in the burn ward on the fourth floor? What's his name?"

"Lucien Furie."

"I'll take you," she said.

Ana came up and took my hand, and Richie walked far enough behind us that you might not think he was walking with us.

It was a lot of stairs to the fourth floor, and the nurse looked at those stairs like they were the last things she wanted to be going up, but she did, breathing like Mother did when she was sick. Finally we got there. It took a couple minutes for the nurse to catch her breath, and the three of us followed her into the double doors of the burn ward.

"I got to go back down, but you talk to Doreen. She can help you."

Me and Ana smiled politely, but Richie couldn't wait for her to leave. He turned to the doors of the burn ward and pushed them open without even looking to see if the nurse was still watching us.

"You ready?" Ana asked me. I knew what she wanted. She was older, she should go first.

"Okay, you go ahead," I said, but she just looked at me.

"No, you," she said.

She never ever admitted that she was scared. I knew I was scared, but I wasn't gonna show it.

"Come on," I said.

The burn ward was divided by white curtains into little spaces, and you had to poke your head in to see people lying in beds wrapped in gauze, with bottles dripping into their arms.

I heard sobbing, but nobody screaming their head off like Lucien was supposed to be doing. I didn't think we were going to find him by opening those white curtains and seeing some people bandaged up like mummies, sometimes a burned hand or foot sticking out from beneath the sheets. I wanted to run, just get out of there. Ava pulled back another curtain, then she turned toward me with her hand over her mouth like she was trying to keep the words from coming out.

"Look!" she said, in a panicky whisper.

"What?" I asked.

"Richie!"

I looked inside, and there was Richie standing behind a man bandaged from head to toe, stretched out on a hospital bed like a statue somebody would get around to standing upright. Richie had a pencil in his hand, and he was jabbing down at the man's face, at his eyes.

"Richie! Let's get! Come on!"

Richie jumped up and down as he stabbed this man, as crazy as a monkey.

"Richie, you don't know who you stabbing!"

"I know!" he said, snarling. He pointed to the man's hands.

"Look at those hands. Nobody here got hands like this man. Nobody's big like this one. He's him."

Richie's pencil snapped as it punctured the bandages over the man's eye. The man didn't flinch.

Blood dotted up in a few places where Richie stuck him, but not much. The man hardly moved. I couldn't see him breathe.

"Auntie thought he was some kind of devil. Look! He don't even care about me sticking him."

Ava pulled out his arm. "Come on, look, this man is dead. You can't hurt a dead man."

"Yes, you can." Richie said.

He pushed Ava away and rolled the bed over to the window.

The bed was heavy and it looked too big for Richie to move. The boy strained so hard, but he got it there to the window, he stood up on it and pushed the windows open.

"Help me get him up!" Richie said.

"No," I said. "He's already dead. You just gonna get in trouble for nothing."

Richie ignored me as he pulled at Lucien's arms. He couldn't get him very far no matter how hard he pulled, then he noticed the belt around the side bars of the bed and Lucien's waist. He tried, but he was so butterfingered he couldn't work the straps loose.

"Help me!" he said.

Ana shook her head, then he looked at me. He started crying and kicking at Lucien's head. Maybe he was right. If this was Lucien, he deserved to suffer more than lying around in bed, even if he was burned up.

Took me a minute to loosen the straps. Then Richie tried to lift him off the bed, but he let go and the body slipped down, landing on top of me.

"Get him off!" I screamed.

I saw Ana's black, shiny shoes as she ran to me. They flipped the body over, and I crawled from under it.

Then the three of us dragged the body the rest of the way to the window.

"You guys pull up on his arms. I'm gonna get under him," Richie said.

When he got that big body a little off the floor, Richie slid under him, and pushing up with his back, he carried him to the open window and got the man's head and shoulders through.

We all shoved until he was hanging there like a blanket drying on a line, half in, half out of the room.

"Yeah, all we got to do is lift his feet and this Cayoodule's gone for good," Richie shouted.

All three of us stood there looking at him, this pig who killed Mother, wondering who would push him over.

I wanted to send him flying down to break his skull on the hard ground, but I couldn't bring myself to do it.

"He's dead," Ana said. "Why we're going throw a dead man out of the window?"

"We've got to get him back," Richie said. "Nobody can say we didn't get him back for what he done."

Richie grabbed his feet and flipped him out of the window. We heard it, a scream coming out of the black hole of mouth as Lucien fell.

"See! I told you he wasn't dead!" Richie shouted.

Richie was right. It felt good. We got Lucien back for what he done Mother.

"What the hell you kids doing!"

It was the nurse! Oh, man, she looked mad! Me and Ava ran to the curtains, knocking them aside until we made it to the hallway. Richie wasn't behind us.

"Wait!" Ava said. "We've got to go back and look for him."

We heard the nurse yell, and then she looked out of the window and screamed. Then we ran as hard as we ever ran. Outside, on the street, we saw all the people gathered around Lucien's bandaged body. We kept going, knowing that nurse would be looking for us.

It took some walking, but we finally found our way back to

35

home. We both wondered if Richie beat us there like he usually did.

"Don't tell Lita nothing," Ana said, like I hadn't already been thinking about that. We weren't going to tell you a thing.

"I'm not saying anything if you don't."

It wasn't like you were our mother and we had to tell you. We didn't have to tell the truth to you. You couldn't make us. We didn't have no mother. And if you didn't have no mother, you had to be grown.

We were grown.

Richie never made it back, but nobody said anything about him getting caught. We expected you shouting to the top of your lungs and us getting a bad beating, soon as you figured out what we had done. The phone rang while I was sitting at the dinner table. I was sure this was gonna be the call to cause us some hurt. Ana kicked me under the table, but I didn't need her telling me what was going on. I pointed to the door, and she nodded. We were running soon as you lifted your heavy hand and we were gonna keep running. Your face showed it. Man, you went pale as a sheet, almost falling out of the chair.

"Somebody did what? Threw him out of a window? When?"

I swear you was gonna faint, but then Big Winston came home, rushing in for dinner, but he knew right away something was wrong.

"The baby? You having it?" he said, in a funny kind of

whisper that sounded more like somebody was strangling him.

"No! It's Lucien."

"What about him? He finally kicked the bucket?"

"Somebody threw him out of the window of the burn ward."

Big Winston took off his cap and ran his hand through his hair.

"Man was just about dead. Why would anybody take the trouble to do that?"

"Somebody who hates him more than I do. I can't imagine anybody could have more hate for that man than me, but . . ."

Then Big Winston looked around the dinner table.

"Hey, where's that boy? He don't miss a meal."

"Yes, where is Richie?" you asked, looking at the both of us.

"I dunno. He said he was going to do some visiting," I said.

Big Winston shrugged. "Yeah? Maybe he's back home." He thought we didn't catch that quick smile he flashed. "You gonna call Aunt Dot and see?" Big Winston asked.

"What for? All that woman does is hang up."

It was funny 'cause the baby started crying and you tried to run to him, but you really couldn't run because you were too big with the next baby. I knew enough not to laugh and make you more mad at me, even if you were waddling like a duck. Not laughing was a whole lot easier than getting the whipping we knew was coming to us.

*T*hen we heard that nurse, that nice colored lady, got blamed for what happened to Lucien. Nobody believed how the nurse said it happened; a colored boy tossed him out of the window of the fourth floor. A big boy with two little white girls with him. That's what we heard you say, and that's when we thought you'd put two plus two together and really beat our behinds.

We thought you had to know and you were up to something. You looked like you knew; your face got red every time you saw us. We were sure you figured it out, but you still didn't get around to beating us. Maybe you were too busy looking for Richie. You'd drop Big Winnie off at the post office and spend the rest of the day with us and the baby in the car as you'd drive all around New Orleans searching for him. Our beating was coming, but we were sure you just wanted us all together to give it to us. We wondered, was it going to be a switch or a strap? Were you going to make us lie across the bed or stand up? Ana said the reason you weren't asking us nothing is you didn't want to hear whatever lie we made up. After a while, waiting for the beating was getting to be worse than the beating.

Remember that day, when it was really hot and muggy, you drove us to Lake Ponchartrain? Wind was blowing hard off the water, whipping our hair till it was crawling around on our heads. You led us down to the edge of the water, and I glanced at Ana and I knew she was thinking what I was thinking, that you were going to try to drown us. The sky was gray, bunched up with jet-black clouds rolling toward us, reminding me of how Mother used to pour a little coffee into our milk. I figured you could drown us and nobody would suspect 'cause the lake looked like it was in a drowning mood. You tried to say something, but the wind was howling now, so it was tough to hear. The baby liked all the commotion and reached out, trying to grab some of that hard air.

"Do you know what happened with Richie?" you shouted.

Your face turned red when we shook our heads.

"So you don't know why Richie ran off? If you don't tell me the truth, I'll slap you both down! So help me God."

Mostly you don't scare me, but you had me scared that time.

"This is serious, so don't give me any lip. Do you know where Richie is?"

We shook our heads.

You looked disgusted, disgusted enough to beat our behinds good.

"I hate trying to get something out of you two. I don't know how Mother handled it. I don't have a clue. Beating you don't matter. Treating you nice don't make a difference, so I'm going to try to talk to you like adults."

I shot a look at Ana. She nodded.

"This is what I hate. You two and that damn secret code. You think nobody else in the world knows what you're up to."

I shrugged for the both of us.

"Listen to me. Don't you ever speak about what you saw. That nurse convinced them she didn't do it. They're looking for a Negro boy and two white girls. If the police find Richie and he talks to them, I don't know what could happen. I don't know what they would do to you two or to Richie. Put you in a home somewhere. Richie, I don't know. They might lock him up in Angola forever."

Ana started crying before me, but pretty soon I was crying

twice as hard, and little Winnie started in too. Then the wind started blowing some hard, and you grabbed our hands and we ran for the car just ahead of the stinging rain.

*Y*ou didn't want us going back to Daddy even though your place was too small for all of us even with Richie gone. Big Winston couldn't get no sleep and would go around the house saying things like "Got people around here like hair on my head" or "Stop making so much dag blasted noise," and all we'd be doing was sitting on the couch reading.

Daddy called and talked to us on the phone, sounding so sweet. I know I wanted to go home, and Ana wanted to go even more than me. I wanted to be back in our own room and to live at home, even if Mother wasn't there.

You couldn't talk us out of it, but you tried.

"It's not going to be the same. Mother is not there, and I'm not either. Daddy don't know how to take care of you. He left that up to me and Mother."

We had our minds made up.

We had each other, and we were big enough to look after each other. You just didn't like the fact we could do it. We didn't need you like how you thought we needed you.

You took us over to Daddy's without saying a word. You wouldn't look at us, and you drove away without waving good-bye, but that didn't bother me. You had to learn we had our own minds.

The house looked all new after the fire. The porch was bigger, with a great big door with a fancy doorbell. We rang it a few

times before we heard footsteps. The door opened, and we expected
to see Daddy there. After not seeing him for so long I was looking forward to it, but it wasn't Daddy standing there. It was
some woman, about your age. She was pretty, really pretty, with
dark skin and long hair, and she had a fresh black eye.

"You must be Doc's girls. I'm Gloria. Pleased to meet
you," she said, without much of a smile. Then she walked out
of the door we just came through and shut it behind her. We
heard Daddy shouting for her from the other room, and I knew
Daddy had just given her that black eye. He came running like
a bull chasing after that woman, but when he saw us, he
looked all confused like somebody had played a trick on him.

"What are you two doing here?"

"We came home," Ana said.

Daddy sighed, putting his hands on his hips.

"Good. I need help with the bar."

We shrugged to each other.

"Get me a beer," Daddy said, rubbing a fresh cut on his
forearm.

I guess Daddy and that girl had it out, and she drew some
blood of her own.

"By the way, did Gloria tell you when she was coming back?"

We both shook our heads, then Daddy rushed out of the
door, chasing after that woman.

Before Daddy enrolled us in school, he showed us how to
run the bar. I was more excited about the bar than the nuns

and going to school, because other than Ana nobody else my age worked in a bar, and we were going to be running it. It was different with Daddy once he started teaching us things. He got serious and expected us to pay attention to everything he was saying and ask questions. I don't ever remember Daddy doing that with us before, paying much attention to what we were doing. We never asked him questions, and he never asked us to ask questions. Mother made it clear that we were to be seen and not heard, but now we could be seen and heard and whatever else because Daddy needed us. The most important thing was how to count back change so nobody could ever beat us out of what they owed us. A beer cost a quarter, a whiskey, fifty cents, that was the important stuff. Daddy spent all afternoon showing us how people try to pull tricks to make you give them back more money than they got coming.

"Never let them make you nervous. Just keep an eye on the money they give you and count it back to them. You can't go wrong."

Once he showed us how to handle the money, Daddy showed where he kept the gun.

"Don't you take nothing from these lowlifes. If they get smart with you, take that gun out and show you mean business." Daddy waved the gun over his head like it was a flag. "Same thing if they get too loud or use cursing words. Get their attention. Tell them to leave, and if they don't, point the gun at them, and if they act a fool shoot them."

He asked us if we had any questions, and then we started working.

That's how it was; when Daddy was off taking a nap, or out

somewhere, we were running the bar and taking care of ourselves. Ana got real good at pool. She started shooting pool out of boredom, but she had a knack for it. She sharpened the knack when she started making quick money off the jokers who came to the bar. None of them believed that this little girl could shoot; they learned their lesson after she emptied their pockets a couple of times. Most of the time we ran the bar all on our own. Gloria, that woman with the black eye, would help sometimes, but I saw her slip money into her pocket more than once, and I guess that's why Daddy gave her black eyes. She looked like she wanted to be anywhere besides with us. Sitting on a stool behind the bar, looking pissed off like watching us sweat was the worse thing she could be doing with herself. Soon enough, she made it clear she didn't like us. We ignored her and Daddy too; we were so busy that they could be having one of their knockdown fights, and we would just step around them and get to it. Ana would work the register, and I'd pour the drinks and serve them. It was pretty easy once we got the hang of it, and it was easy to find time to do homework because since Mother died, the bar was a lot emptier. People complained Daddy watered down the drinks too much. It was true, we spent lots of time soaping bottles down and scrubbing off the labels and putting on new ones. Daddy said to throw out anybody who said anything about the quality of the liquor. This one old drunk thought he could scare us into giving him another drink by shouting that we were serving "piss water," but he got the message when Ana pulled the gun out of the drawer and pointed it at him.

"You better get out of here, or I'm going to shoot you, yeah!"

"She will!" I added.

The drunk left, and word got around that we were just like Mother; don't mess with us unless you wanted a whole lot of trouble.

We were supposed to go to school and come right to the bar, but mostly Daddy tried to keep us home. He'd get our work from the nuns, and come into the bar shrugging like it was no big deal. He'd toss our homework onto a table, smiling like he was Santa Claus, like he brought us the best gift in the world. We had to be two of the sickest girls in all of New Orleans. Sometimes we would miss a week of school because of Daddy partying too hard and being too hungover to get the bar open. He'd tell those nuns we had Indian fire or measles, then the chicken pox; we had the chicken pox ten times. He kept that up until they just about gave up on us. The way things were going, we were going to have to repeat the fourth grade. Daddy said there was nothing he could do about it.

"I can't be hiring no more people. The bar don't make money the way it used to. Maybe one of you could go to school at a time. You're twins. Nobody can tell who's who anyway. You know, trade off."

We tried that. I'd go to school and bring home the lesson, and then so would Ana. We could do that only when Daddy or Gloria were working. Even though we missed so much school, we did good; we both got A's on everything. Schoolwork was easy. The nuns gave us harder stuff, but we got A's on that too. At first the nuns thought we were cheating, but we showed them when they

44

tried to trick us. They made me take a test without Ana, and I got an A just like Ana. We did all they asked right in front of them. They didn't understand how we were. If Ana could do something like write a nice letter, I had to do it better. If she read a book, I had to read it faster; that was us. There was nothing they could teach us in school that we couldn't learn on our own better.

45

*D*addy made Gloria take us to get summer clothes. We didn't want her to go with us, but Daddy said he was too busy. Gloria wasn't happy about it at all, but that might of had to do with the new black eye she had.

Ana kicked my shin when I asked Gloria about it; Gloria just shrugged.

"I walked into the door," she said.

That's what she told us last time. We knew Daddy was beating her up every now and then, just like he used to do Mother. That's how we knew he liked her. If he didn't like her, he would have thrown her out after he beat her up the first time. Ana didn't like her much, but I didn't mind her. Daddy was happy, and that made him easy to live with.

Gloria didn't know nothing about shopping. She took us where poor people get their clothes on some stinky street where everybody kept staring at us 'cause we were so light-skinned and they were dark. The shop she took us to had clothes in bundles and heaps on the floor. People were picking through them and Gloria looked at us like we were supposed to find something in all that mess.

"Mother never bought us clothes off of some dirty floor, no. We go to stores where they had mannequins and people who talk to you about what you want."

"Well, your daddy said to take you to get clothes, but he didn't give me no money for that kind of fancy."

Ana whispered to me, "I saw Daddy give her money. She's trying to keep it."

That's when I asked Gloria how much he gave her. She shrugged like she didn't understand what I was saying.

"Daddy gave you some money. How much?" I asked again.

"Two dollars," she said, looking away.

"We're gonna ask soon as we get home. I know Daddy gave you more money to spend than that," Ana said, talking to Gloria like she was just a big liar.

Gloria raised her hand like she wanted to hit Ana, but Ana didn't flinch. We didn't have to say nothing else, but she knew we caught her red-handed. She didn't want Daddy to black her other eye.

"Alright! You two too smart for your own good."

Then she walked out of that shop and back to the trolley. We went to real stores and found clothes Mother would have wanted us to have, not something a ragpicker would wear.

Aunt Odie came by, and she had candy for us, chocolates for me and those chewy caramel things Ana liked. It wasn't our birthday, but she wanted to take us to get a toy.

"You children have endured so much, you deserve something," she said seriously. Aunt Odie always talked serious. When you first saw her she looked scary, but she was always nice to us. Treating us every time she'd see us like she was a skinny and dark Santa Claus. We were surprised to see her because she didn't come over much because she hated Daddy. It wasn't no secret. Aunt Odie couldn't stand Daddy. She wouldn't stay in the same room with him. Daddy always made fun of her. When we were on our way to see Aunt Odie, Daddy would say mean things.

"So, y'all going to see what the cat drug in? Don't know why my daughters have to go see the ugliest witch in the South."

Daddy never tried to stop us from seeing Aunt Odie if every blue moon she showed up. We knew why. We could tell from how he looked when he talked about her. She scared him good.

We were running the bar for Daddy until he was supposed to come back from doing errands. We couldn't leave, specially with so many people in the bar with a big thirst on a hot day.

"Don't worry about this bar. I'll take care of this," Aunt Odie said. She turned around and clapped her hands so loud it sounded like a gunshot.

"Go! Get out! Now!" She boomed.

Me, I thought they'd just ignore her and go back to drinking like they do until you stop serving them, but I was wrong. Maybe those bums and drunks didn't look at Aunt Odie when she came in, or they saw her in the corner of they eye and didn't look at her again. After that booming shout they had to look at her face, and they had to see how she looked like a mahogany skeleton dressed in white with just a little layer of skin covering that lanky body. And they saw that face of hers that looked like a grinning skull. They cleared out of the bar in no time.

"Daddy's gonna be mad," Ana said.

"Don't you worry about your father. When he brings himself back here, I'll tell him what I did and what I'm going to do."

We could tell Aunt Odie was furious. She was mad at Daddy, and she was always mad at Daddy.

She took us to the toy store, and I got a pretty doll and Ana picked out a guitar.

After she bought us ice cream and we were going back home, Aunt Odie told us what she planned to do.

"I'm going to shoot your father."

"Huh?" Ana said, but she heard her like I did.

"Your father is a bad man, and he shouldn't be raising you. He's no father. If you had no father, you would be better off. You two should be with Lita. She's your mother now."

Ana licked her ice cream and acted like she wasn't listening.

"You shouldn't be staying at that house. Can't you feel it? What happened there has to have time to die down. And I don't know how long that take. Lucien isn't the end of it, but that house is awash with his evil."

Aunt Odie sagged on the trolley bench, looking not just furious but worried as well. Usually she didn't talk with her hands, but her hands twisted about as though she was trying to draw a picture of what she was trying to say. It wasn't any clearer.

"The house is suffering. Don't you feel it? Do you hear it?"

I shook my head, and so did Ana. I didn't know what she

was talking about. Houses don't suffer, they just fall down or somebody sets them on fire. People suffer. We suffered bad when Mother died. The house didn't care, and the house didn't know. Aunt Odie had some strange ideas.

"I know you two don't understand about the spirits, about how the spirits walk through this world to the next, but believe me when I tell you that Helen's spirit is still there in that house."

I brightened up just like Ana did when we heard that, but Aunt Odie shook her head to correct us.

"Helen's spirit is there because she's trying to protect you from the other things, the other spirits, the Mal spirits, that want to harm you. That's why you must leave, and soon."

I looked at Ana, and she looked at me like some weird funhouse mirror, reflecting back just how scared I was. Just a second ago I was happy to be home, but Aunt Odie made that seem really silly.

When we arrived at the house, somebody had already opened the bar, and if it wasn't Gloria there was gonna be a whole lot of mess. Daddy would be mad, madder than a wet hen. Just a mess. We let Aunt Odie walk to the bar, and she stuck her head in and we heard Daddy shout a string of curses.

"What the hell! What the hell you doing here! What did you do with my girls? Did you tell them to close down the bar? I sure in the hell hope you didn't do that!" he said, shouting so loud it made my ears hurt. Daddy's face was twisted up in a ugly sneer. We backed up, looking for a place to hide. Daddy wasn't heavy-handed with us. He didn't bother with that, but we always did what he said. The one thing he really wanted from us was to keep the bar open. We didn't do it, and I don't know if Aunt Odie could stop whatever beating Daddy wanted to give us.

We saw Daddy shake his fist at Aunt Odie.

"You better calm yourself and shut your mouth before I do it for you," Aunt Odie said.

"You ugly heifer! Who told you to mess around in my business?"

Daddy kept coming toward Aunt Odie. She stood her ground, that white sack of a dress whipping around her flagpole-skinny legs.

"You think I'm scared of you 'cause you think you some kind of witch?"

Daddy was about to do something hurtful to Aunt Odie, rolling up his sleeves and gritting his teeth, but he must of thought better about it because his feet started to slow.

He stopped. Was he thinking about it, taking on Aunt Odie? She was tall and scary, but she was just an old lady.

Then Daddy shook his head like he was waking up from a nap. He lunged at her with his hands reaching for her throat.

"Daddy, don't!" we both yelled.

He stopped again, but not because of us. The little gun Aunt Odie pulled from that sack purse she carried did the trick.

Daddy gritted his teeth, but he didn't close his eyes. He dared her to shoot him.

"I told you I'm not scared of you. If you're going to do it, do it!"

Aunt Odie hesitated. I think she even lowered the gun for a

second. Daddy smiled, and his chest stuck out a little more, like he knew he had won.

Then Odie pointed the gun at him again and pulled the trigger.

The gun didn't sound like any gun I ever heard. It made a little popping noise, not too much louder than a toy.

Daddy's eyes were big as saucers. He looked down at his chest to see if he was hit, then Aunt Odie shot him again.

He tried to run, but Odie had them long legs, and she took big steps and kept after him, shooting all the time. Daddy did a funny dance, running straight ahead but twisting aside like he was trying to slip through a tight space. Finally he rolled over on the ground and covered his head.

"Stop! Please stop! You shot me enough already!"

Daddy stayed on the ground and Aunt Odie stood above him, staring down at him like yesterday's trash.

"Let those girls go to their big sister, or next time I'm gonna use my gun with real bullets."

Aunt Odie waved one of her big hands at us, and she took off as fast as those longs legs could carry her.

Daddy never said nothing about what happened that day. He just took a long soak in the tub to calm his nerves.

We went in and started back to work. The bar filled up quickly, not with the usual drunks but with neighbors we hardly ever seen. Word had got around about Daddy getting shot and walking away from it.

"Heard your daddy was shot twenty times and he didn't bleed?" Miss Rita, who worked at the funeral home, asked. She wanted to know everything—like all those other people staring at me and Ana like we had nothing better to do but tell them our business.

"No, she shot him six times with blanks," I said.

Miss Rita didn't want to hear that.

"When I heard he got shot, I knew we were gonna have a big funeral. But I should have known it all along. Your daddy is in league with the devil. You can't kill somebody like that. You got to let the devil take them."

I started to cry. He might do bad things, but he was still our daddy.

Rita looked confused, like she had done wrong by us but didn't know what to do about it.

"Look, sugar, I don't mean to say your daddy's working for the devil. I just mean it's not every day you hear about somebody like him getting shot and he don't get a scratch on him."

I guess she didn't hear my words. Grown-ups look at you like they're listening, but they hear what they want. I figured the devil would take care of his own, and she was mad 'cause she couldn't make money burying Daddy like she did Mother. She'd just have to wait her turn and not be greedy.

Ana kicked me awake with her big feet, whispering about something, but she had been doing that all week, so I was used to it.

"What?"

She whispered some more, but I still couldn't hear what she was saying.

"What?" I asked again, and she clasped her hand over my mouth.

Before I could bite her palm, she spoke up enough for me to understand.

"Hear it?"

"I don't hear a thing. You keep waking me up about hearing something and I keep hearing nothing."

"Listen!"

"Okay," I said, and cocked my ear like I could hear whatever she thought she was hearing, and I started to fall back to sleep.

Screaming. A woman screaming. A man screaming. I woke up trying to catch my breath.

"What, you heard it?" Ana asked.

Then I felt it, like it was raining tears. Sadness. Sad like when Mother died. I looked at Ana. She felt it too.

"What's that?" I asked.

"We're feeling something we're not supposed to."

We pulled the covers over our heads and tried waiting till the sadness went away, but then we heard pounding and roughhousing like there was a big fight going on in the hallway.

"Somebody's fighting Daddy," I said.

"Can't be Aunt Odie. She's over the lake."

I slipped out of bed and without putting on my robe went to the dresser drawer and took out the gun.

"We got to go see," I said.

"I'm not going out there," Ana said.

She was trembling. I was scared too, but I had to see. I reached for the doorknob and tried to turn it, but the metal burned my hand like I had it on a hot frying pan.

"My hand! My hand's burned up!"

Ana grabbed it and forced it open. I didn't want to see, so I kept my eyes closed.

54

"Nothing's wrong with you. Your hand ain't burned."

I opened my eyes and looked. It looked just the same.

"Some kind of trick," Ana said.

I shook my head and walked to the door and tried it, but this time I did it quick.

I flung the door open and rushed into the hallway. I expected to see Daddy fighting somebody. The hall was empty.

"See!" Ana said, from behind me. "This place is haunted, like Aunt Odie said."

Then from up ahead, where the fire that burned down the house started, we saw flames.

Blam!

We both jumped at the sound of a gunshot. I was so scared I had pulled the trigger.

"Run!" Ana said, and we hurried back to our bedroom and slammed the door shut.

But the room was filling up with smoke, and we both started to choke, and the sadness got thicker than the smoke. Choking and crying, we both collapsed to the floor, calling out to Mother.

"Stop your crying," I heard Ana say, but it wasn't Ana.

All the smoke and noise and heat, all of that stopped.

I reached for Ana's hand, then we opened our eyes and saw Mother. Her arms—they were cut and bleeding, but it didn't bother her. She smiled at us and waved liked she was watching us leaving on a train.

"Listen to Lita. She knows what's best for you. Now go back to sleep."

She watched us crawl back to bed, and then she walked to the door and disappeared through it. We fell asleep in each other's arms.

It wasn't a dream.

Nobody can dream like that. Dreaming about what you want chases it away.

Mother, she came to us.

5

Lita

That was the first time I heard about Mother appearing, and I wasn't happy to hear about it then and I wasn't happy to hear about it again ten years later. If Mother was sending messages from the next world, why hadn't I received one? I didn't believe it anyway. It was just nonsense, but Ava told me all that for a reason. She wanted me to know her side of the story so that I would treat her like an equal. I was supposed to step aside and let that cheeky brat live like a woman because she thought she was one.

When she finished her long-winded tale, I patted her shoulder and walked away.

Her eyes were on me as I set the table. I wanted to see how far she'd go, if she thought she could stare me down while not lifting a finger to help with dinner. My temper bubbled up.

"Ava, take yourself to your room. You're not grown no matter how much you think you are. There's only one woman in this house, and that's me."

I watched her swing her hips as she rushed out of the kitchen.

Yeah, I already had a plateful of problems, but God must have thought I had an appetite for more.

Ava started drawing men like a bucket of spoiled milk draws flies. Oh, yes, I felt like I was seeing a movie I had seen before.

The knocks started coming. More than one idiot appeared at the door with flowers in hand proposing marriage; some handsome, others ugly, young or old, with money or without. A bunch of losers who saw everything they needed to survive in this life in the abundance of Ava's body. I remember one, a damned undertaker who wore drab clothes but nice, shiny shoes to match the shininess of his pockmarked face (maybe he thought corpses looked stylish), rushed through his words like he didn't have a moment to spare.

"My name is Guy Jones, and I own the Freeman's Mortuary on Slausion. I'd like to talk to you about your daughter."

I didn't bother to correct him that she was my sister and not my daughter. Somehow I got curious about this one.

"What do you need to talk about?"

"I want to marry your daughter."

I looked him up and down with contempt.

"How old are you?"

"I'm twenty-eight."

What an ugly, lying vulture! He was at least ten years older than twenty-eight.

"Mr. Johnson, do you know how old this girl you're interested is?"

"Eighteen?"

I shook my head.

"Seventeen?"

"Yeah."

"I'll be damned."

"Yeah, maybe so," I said and slammed the door in his face.

He knocked again.

"Listen," he said, wringing his hands together as if he had a invisible rag.

"I know she's underage, but if we could work something out, maybe that would do it. You know?"

"You know, what?"

He smiled at me with his shiny face glaring in the afternoon sun.

"If I give you a hundred dollars?"

"Hold still, mister. I'll be right back."

Swearing under my breath, I shut the door.

He should have thanked God that I wasn't cooking, because I might have had a pot of hot grease or boiling water in my hands and he would have been dead. I found the broom near the door, grabbed onto it and rushed outside with that broom cocked over my head like a caveman's club.

He raised his arms to shield his face, but I brought the broom down on top of his head so hard that it shattered in my hands. His legs splayed and he parked hard on his butt, grimacing like he busted something. I whacked him once more with the handle; his eyes rolled up into his head, and he toppled over.

But I wasn't having any part of this bastard stretched out on my lawn like he was taking a nap, so I turned the hose on and aimed a cold stream at him. He woke, shaking his head like a bewildered dog.

"Get up! Go! Don't let me see you around here again."

Then Ava turned the corner, walking home from school, holding her books right below her chest, I bet to boost that ample bosom of hers a bit further up. She hardly batted an eye as she walked by, seeing me, hose in one hand, broken broom in the other, in another red-faced rage.

She watched me hose that fool man off the lawn with so little interest, he could have been a stray dog turd.

"See!" I shouted. "This is the kind of trouble you bring. This is all your fault!"

"Who's he?" she said, at the hastily retreating mortician.

I shook my head in disbelief.

"That's one of your suitors."

Ava wrinkled her face in disgust.

"I don't know that man," she said, and without a backward glance she walked into the house. I turned off the hose and tossed the broken broom into the trash.

*W*inston came in from the garage, wiping oil off his hands with a rag stained with it.

"Take your shoes off. You know you got oil on them."

Winston frowned, and after another minute of wiping his hands, he tossed that nasty rag onto the counter and bent down to unlace them. A socket wrench fell from his coverall pocket and landed on the floor with a thud.

"What, Lita?"

"Come here and see for yourself."

He followed me to the living room and pulled back the curtains of the big window.

"See!"

He slipped his head by mine and looked out toward the street.

One thing about the neighborhood is that it was neat and clean, with clipped lawns and hedges, even if the people were just as crazy as down in New Orleans, maybe even more so. I pointed to a run-down station wagon parked almost directly in front of our house and the very big man leaning against it.

"See what?"

"The man! You see him, he's right there."

Winston shook his head.

"What? He needs some work done?"

"I don't know. He's just been waiting around, staring at the house. It's Ava. He's waiting on her like all these other men that come around here like she's some bitch in heat."

Winston sighed and turned back to the window and squinted.

"You don't really know if he's waiting on Ava."

"He's waiting on Ava."

Winston whistled low and long.

"You need to do something about it."

Winston's face clouded up. He started to work his hands as though he was still holding the oil rag.

"Yeah, like what?"

"Talk to him."

"Talk to him?"

"Yes, that's what I said. I speak clearly, don't I? You go out there and find out this man's intentions."

"You want me to tangle with this big monkey over that sister of yours? What if he knocks my block off?"

I opened the door and held it, gesturing for him to get to it.

"Nobody's gonna knock your block off."

I didn't say, except for me . . . but he got the point and stepped outside onto the porch. There's only about ten yards between the street and our porch, but Winston made it seem like Moses wandering in the desert, curlicuing about like he was some kind of damn bumblebee stopping at every rosebush, deadheading spent blooms and trimming unhealthy leaves with his pocket knife, then squatting down to pick at the crabgrass he had missed in his last inspection.

Maybe Winston was hoping the man would get so bored he'd drive off. Just when I was ready to throw open the door and send this guy on his way, Winston managed to meander over to him, I guess, thinking he was being casual. Winston said something, and the man smiled, or maybe sneered at him.

He must have been six-six, made Winston look like a little boy dressed up as a mechanic.

They walked around to the front of the car, and the man reached his hand under the front grille, popped the hood, and lifted it up. Winston leaned over and looked inside at the engine and immediately begin tinkering.

Oh, for crying out loud! We got some kind of child molester hanging around in front of our house, and he's going to work on his car. It drives me crazy—I've got to do everything that makes any sense when it comes to the family.

I walked up to the car with my broom in hand. The big man smiled at me like I was about to start sweeping out his front seat.

Winston was so startled to see me, he hit his head on the hood.

"Lita, what are you doing out here?"

"Checking on you. Aren't you supposed to be doing something for me?"

Winston shrugged and turned to the man.

"This is Milford. Ava told him I was a mechanic and I'd fix his car for free," Winston said, scowling as he pronounced "free" like it was the worst kind of insult.

Milford smiled at me and stuck out his hand.

"Hi, ma'am. I'm Milford. I'm on the spirit squad with Ava."

"Yeah? I used to be a cheerleader in high school," I said, without intending to.

"Ava told me she could help me get my car fixed if I came by."

"Sure, my husband is a good mechanic," I replied, feeling like a huge weight had been lifted off me. This big man, who looked like anybody's football player, a boxer, a wrestler, something, was a fruit. His voice was higher than mine, and he stood there with a shirt so tight his arms looked like they would burst the sleeves if he flexed. He had them crossed across his shoulders like you only see girls do. What got me was his arched eyebrows; but I guess when you're built like he was, not too many people would want to poke fun at you.

"Could you help me out?" he asked Winston.

Winston's eyes got big as plates. Maybe if the man had been a murderer or a molester, he might have felt more at ease than him being a fairy.

"Seems to me you need a water pump."

"Yeah?"

"You can pick that up at Pep Boys. Won't take you no time to fix it."

"I don't know how to fix cars."

Winston shook his head, not bothering to disguise his contempt.

"Don't you worry, my husband will fix your car. You just pull around to the alley, and he'll get on it."

Milford clapped his big hands together. He got into that bucket of bolts and drove it carefully toward the alley.

Winston's eyes flared. He couldn't wait to rip into me.

"What? I'm supposed to fix his car?"

"Yes, you are."

"He can fix his own damn car. Anybody could fix a water pump. You just unscrew the old one and screw on the new one."

"Good, you can do it."

"Lita, I do a lot of things you tell me to, but one thing is for sure, I'm not hanging around in an alley with some fruit a foot taller than me and outweighs me by a hundred pounds."

"Winston, you go get that part. I'll stay with Milford."

I didn't have much convincing to do with Winston. He rushed over to his Galaxie 500 and made a fast U-turn, driving away in a burst of exhaust and burned rubber.

I walked around through the yard, pushing aside the dogs, Music and Crystal, beagle hunting dogs that Winston paid top dollar for and then never used to hunt. I opened the door of Winston's paradise, a cluttered nightmare of a mess of a garage, unlocked the garage door, and pushed it up and open.

Milford had pulled his car close to the garage but had the engine off.

"It started to overheat," he said in that sweet voice of his.

Now that I had the garage open, Milford began to push the car up the sharp incline into the garage.

"I could help," I said.

"Don't you bother," he said, not even breathing hard.

Afterward, he wiped his face with a handkerchief and caught his breath.

"So you and Ava are friends?"

"Oh, yeah. She's a young woman, you know, mature. Not silly like most girls. We talk."

"Then you must know about these men hounding her."

Milford laughed. "You know about that?"

"Yes, just last week I beat a man with a broom for coming around here."

"You do that a lot?"

"All the time," I said, sighing.

"You shouldn't worry. She's a good girl. Not like some of those tramps trying to catch every man they see."

That was a relief to hear. I half expected Ava to come home with news I dreaded to hear—that she was pregnant.

"Listen, I'm glad you and Ava are friends."

Milford's eye's brightened.

"We're best friends! No lie. You know some girls get snooty and try to make fun 'cause I want to be Yell King, I don't care. I know who I am, and I know what I want to do."

"That's right."

"Ava's not like that. She accepts you for who you are."

I nodded, having to bite my lip. It suddenly seemed funny to me that we would be standing around in the garage talking about Milford's future in cheerleading.

"And she don't get into your business."

"No."

"I love your sister, and I would do anything for her."

"You need to do something for me," I slipped in. "Watch out for Ava."

Milford shrugged.

"She in some kind of trouble?"

"Not trouble. No, it's just that trouble is gonna find

her. Trouble is bound to happen. At least, that's what I feel in my bones."

Milford looked alarmed. That's what I wanted. To see if he really did have feelings for her, and if he would keep her pretty behind out of hot water.

"Ma'am, you don't got to worry. I watch out for all the girls. Boys sometimes think they can push me around like I'm some punk. I might act silly sometimes, but when I have to, I can jump out of my silliness and into my man-ness and knock some fool out."

"Come on, let's go to the kitchen," I said. "Get you a Coke."

In that short time of knowing Milford, I came to like him a lot. Even the crazy hounds took to him; instead of barking and biting at his heels, the dogs nudged and nipped each other out of the way so Milford could pet them.

Inside, after setting him up with potato chips, we talked about drinks. He wanted a Strawberry Crush, but all I had was cola. Then he talked of homemade root beer like it was holy water. I told him something about our background; how Mother died, and me getting the girls, and how hard it was dealing with Ava's too-quick womanhood. I had the poor young man shaking his head.

"Yes, ma'am, you got a whole lot to worry about. I can see that with my own eyes."

"I'm just hoping she don't get silly. If she gets silly, then God knows," I said.

"Yeah, she's a keg of dynamite. I see boys lining up to talk to her; they follow her around like she's Cleopatra."

I shrugged. "If you get word to me about what's going on, if some creepy man tries to pick her up, if you could try to stop her. . . . I know it's a lot, but I'd be obligated. You keep an eye on her, and I'll make sure you get your car fixed."

Milford reached his big hand over and patted mine.

"Don't you worry, I'll take care of it. I'm gonna be a secret agent for you."

"Thanks," I said, so grateful for his reassurance.

"I don't think your husband likes me much."

"Don't pay no attention to that man. There's nothing that he likes too much; not the yolk of a egg, the jelly in a jelly doughnut, or the garlic in pot roast. Don't you worry about him, or it'll drive you crazy."

Milford doubled over with laughter so loud and abrupt I had to cover my ears.

"Ma'am, you too funny."

I heard the front door being unlocked; Winston came in, scowling like he was about to shoot the dog, back from buying the water pump. He took another look at Milford, grunted, and headed out of the kitchen to the garage.

"Oh, yeah, your husband don't like me one bit."

"Milford, I like you, and Ava likes you. What my husband likes, when it comes down to it, don't mean a hill of beans to me."

*D*on't *get me* wrong, on the right day, when the weather's cool and crisp and you can see the mountains and the Hollywood sign, and you're on your way to make groceries, and you smell jasmine, peaches, and lemons, or you're at the beach and see waves burst up onto the shore, I love that about this Los Angeles. It's the people I can't stand.

In New Orleans I knew where I stood. I was colored, even if I looked white. I belonged with the colored. In Los Angeles it isn't like that. L.A. is the size of ten New Orleanses. People don't know your brown-skinned sister, or your black-as-coal uncle. You stand on your own. Every day when I went to work and drove out of my black neighborhood, I became a white woman, white as anyone could ever want to be. It wasn't like passing; passing involved risk, but in Los Angeles there wasn't risk. You were what you looked like. I had the skills people wanted; data-entry training. Finding job offers was too easy, like picking lemons in Los Angeles, they were all over. I never brought up the fact that I was a colored woman, and they didn't ask about it, except for this one cracker interviewing me who wanted to know about my address, what kind of neighborhood I lived in. He was smooth, I'll give him that. If it wasn't for his nasty, toothy smile, I might not have noticed. He was on to me. Either I was passing or I was married to a colored man, both unacceptable to this interviewer.

I knew it then; I wouldn't get that job, or if I did, he'd try to extract a price for his silence, my dignity or more. I smiled at this asshole, knowing exactly what he was thinking, that he was smarter than me, better than me. All this secret bullshit. He asked me about my neighborhood once more.

"Lita, now where do you live again?"

I surprised myself and began to cry.

"Take your stinking job and shove it where the sun don't shine," I said, loud enough for the whole office of starched-down white folks to hear, and they heard me all right, all that shock on their faces made me feel good as I walked to my car. Whatever fear of white people I had in New Orleans was gone in Los Angeles. Now, as white as anybody, I could curse them out, and what would be the consequence? White people had the right to scream at each other, and I was going to use that right for all it was worth.

I rushed home and told Winston how I cursed out a white man in front of a office filled with white people and that it felt damn good.

"Lita, you can't do that. That's nothing but trouble."

"It wasn't trouble for me," I said. "It was easy, and it felt good. I want to do it again if some white trash wants to embarrass me."

"Don't do it. Don't be causing problems. This ain't New Orleans."

I didn't bother to respond. That's how Winston was raised, and it was as much a part of him as the hair on his head. Don't draw attention to yourself. Be a fly on the wall. Be a shadow on the floor; just don't give white people a chance to get a bead on you. Down in New Orleans that made sense, but L.A. was different—at least, that's what I thought at the time.

I did find the job I wanted, one where everyone thought I was the attractive white woman from Louisiana who didn't have much to say, who didn't have any interest in having a drink after work. It was all I could hope for; I got paid more than I had ever been paid, and I was treated well, like white people. If it meant I couldn't have pictures of my brown-skinned kids on the desk, that was okay. I could accept that to put food on the table. I knew the moment I got sick of that job I could tell all of them to kiss my ass. I'd find another job, just as good, in a week.

Now, though, my life had reversed; driving home to my neighborhood brought a new kind of attention. Police stopped me on more than one occasion. Once I was pulled over by this cop who looked like he stepped out of a television show; close-cropped hair, sunburned white face, walking to the car scrutinizing me at the window, taking off sunglasses and speaking in a low voice so as not to be overheard. This cop was there to steer me straight.

"Listen, lady. I pulled you over because you don't belong in this neighborhood."

"Excuse me," I said, confused at what he was getting at. Then it was clear as day.

"This is a black neighborhood. You lost? Follow me out."

"No . . . thanks. I'm visiting friends."

The cop raised an eyebrow.

"Friends, huh? I guess you know what you're doing."

The cop turned around and walked to the patrol car without a look back.

Nigger lover.

That's what was weird about my life in Los Angeles; everybody saw me as they wanted to see me.

The Spanish people talked to me in Spanish, whites thought I was white. Colored people took a minute or two to add it up, trying to figure out what was my angle, then they got it, thought about their cousin who looked white. It was interesting in a way, not belonging anywhere; floating unmoored.

Cousin Benny had moved his family out to Riverside and told them never to say what they were, or where they came from—at least, that was the tale chasing after him. Did he tell them to forget what they were, or maybe it was what they used to be? Anyway, it was their own business and not mine. I guess Benny had decided I was good enough or light enough to visit them, because he called repeatedly, insisting that I come. He hadn't seen anyone from New Orleans in ages. I took my youngest, Jude, out there to visit because he was my darkest, and I wanted to see their reaction to him. Benny and his wife were happy to see me, but they rushed Jude into the house like he was a bank robber and the cops were right on his butt. I knew exactly what was going on, that they had made that leap, across the river of race, but still Benny was worried that the hint of brown in my child's skin could ruin it all.

Benny had married a white woman; he had a beautiful house and a job as a pharmacist. His kids were two blond boys with straight hair and hazel eyes. My Jude had curly hair and a tan, a permanent tan, and that was unacceptable. They needed to be whiter than their neighbors to pull it off. I guess Benny thought that I was of the same mind, but that was the difference between me and Benny; he wanted to belong, needed to belong, had ambitions of a colorless life of plenty. I just wanted people to respect me, or leave me the hell alone.

Benny's kids seemed nice enough, but I realized as I talked to them that they had little to do with the other children in the neighborhood. Benny kept them in; both boys were pale like the sickest of shut-ins. It made sense; Benny didn't want them to slip up and give it away that they were Negroes, so he kept them inside, growing like mushrooms in a hothouse basement.

Benny tried to encourage me to move out to Riverside, that it was a lot easier than Los Angeles, there was nobody to hold you back. I wonder if he meant black people or white.

I realized that Winston and I weren't going to make it. For him the world was frightening, and you had to walk softly to keep it from tearing your head off and chewing you up like some cat with a cornered mouse. But I wasn't some damn mouse. I wasn't frightened.

I was angry.

Angry that so much of my life was spent retreating, running, and pretending, trying to find some peace of mind.

It always gets crazier, like the whole damn world was set on driving me into the ground or out of my shitting mind. No; I might feel like I'm slipping under dark waters, but I won't. If it came down to it, I'd rather be a hammer than a nail. Let somebody be afraid of me.

I'll give them a damn good reason to be.

Winston couldn't believe I wanted a divorce. At first he laughed, smirking like I was making a sick joke; then it sunk in. I never saw Winston cry, he cried. I tried to wave the whole thing off, as though he was right, that I was just messing with him. It didn't work; he knew I was serious.

The kids knew I was unhappy and barely could stand to listen to their father. We argued like that was conversation. If we couldn't say it shouting at each other, it didn't get said. Now that I was making as much money as Winston or more, I listened to him even less. It pained me to hear his opinions about everything—notions about soap, Lava versus Borax; white gravy being better than brown; how the boys should be disciplined (a wet towel leaves no marks); how he should wake us up in the morning, cupping his hands to play a ear-blasting revelry.

But it was when he decided that a nun, Sister Patrell, was right about Jude—that our boy was slow—that settled it for me.

*T*hink about that, I married a man who wouldn't stand up for his own children.

Winston told me this after he got off from the graveyard shift at the post office, waking me up from a deep sleep with this shit. He must have thought he was doing me a favor, breaking this news down to me slowly like I couldn't handle the truth all at once. Once he got around to making sense, I sat there, moving from the thickness of sleep into a slow boil to rage.

"She said Jude is retarded?" I asked, shaking my head.

"She said something about the boy needing to stay back in the first grade."

"And you didn't slap this sister down? Don't you see it for yourself? He's your son, too. Jude is plenty smart. He reads, he can add. He writes his name. What the hell a boy in the first grade is supposed to know?"

"Now, Lita."

"Now, Lita, my ass! You don't let somebody run down your own flesh and blood. I don't care if this woman is a nun; she's a bitch."

"Lita, leave it alone."

"Oh, yeah, I'll leave it be when I put my foot up that nun's ass."

"Lita! Why do you have to talk like that!"

"Oh, shut up, Winston. I'll curse if I fucking feel like it."

"Well, you didn't curse like that in New Orleans."

"What are you saying, California makes me curse?"

Winston shook his head in disgust. "California changed you. You don't act like the same person I married in New Orleans. You curse like a sailor, and you let yourself go."

Let myself go? Why not just say it? I got heavy. What did he expect? With all that I had to do, who has time to take care of themselves? It's a miracle that I can comb my hair in the morning.

"Why don't you be man enough to say what you mean? You think I got fat."

"I'm not talking about that."

"Yes, you are. Stop lying."

"Lita, you just picking fights."

"You just didn't know me in New Orleans. That's all. For that matter you don't know me now! You think I'm happy, having to live the way you want me to live? Listening to your bullshit like it's gospel?"

Those words must have stung him, because he shrugged in disgust and barged out of the door.

Soon as my anger cooled, I wondered what the hell I was supposed to do now. Find a lawyer? Start the divorce? Should I take off work and go up to the Holy Name of Jesus Christ and tell that nun where to get off? Could I make it on my own, supporting two boys? Then there was Ava—what was I supposed to do with her?

Then I thought about that nun and how easy she had it. No husband driving you crazy, no kids pulling you apart; a life of quiet and solitude; a reasonable life. This nun had all of that. Holy my ass, she probably spent her time lying in bed eating chocolates, conjuring up new ways she could humiliate kids.

*A*va *didn't come* home from cheerleading practice. She knew the rules. She needed to have her butt home by eight o'clock, or it would get beat.

Not a call with a preposterous lie—"We got locked inside of the gym and couldn't get out."

No, nothing like that, but being too distracted to pay attention to much else but getting dinner ready and making sure Jude had a bath and was ready for school in the morning, I lost track of time, or maybe I just wanted her out of my mind. Just that sense that things were wrong and out of hand, but that was how it was most of the time, and I had learned how to ignore it.

"Mama, where's Ava?" Jude asked, knocking at my bedroom door.

The boy probably wanted his good-night kiss from his aunt and couldn't sleep.

"Shit! It's ten-thirty! Where the hell is she!" I shouted, and Jude ran out of the room like I was after him with a belt. I found the boy cowering in the hall closet.

Jude shrugged, relieved not to be in trouble. I returned to my bedroom and searched through my purse until I found the paper with Milford's address on it. He didn't have a phone, and he lived in the Jungle, the tropical-theme apartments at the foot of Baldwin Hills. I didn't want to go to the Jungle at night; one street would be fine, safe as could be, but you turned the corner, and you took your life in your hands.

After checking on Winston Jr., who was sleeping like a log, I told Jude to go back to bed. When he was finally snoring, I hurried out to the car.

It was a short drive to Milford's apartment building. He lived close to La Brea in a block of apartments with palms and flowers all about the front. I exhaled; Milford lived on a nice street.

I reached into my shoulder bag and felt the reassuring handle of the cleaver I had brought along with me. I walked into the complex, past a swimming pool that was lit from beneath, and even late at night I heard voices, conversations from by the pool, smelled cigarette smoke. Everything was tranquil, but I couldn't relax; my nails dug into the flesh of my palms as I hurried by a blur of apartment numbers.

79

Finally Milford's apartment appeared, but I hesitated and strained to hear the voices from behind the door, then I heard his. I knocked.

A minute later Milford opened the door, shirtless, in a pair of cutoff jeans. Behind him I saw another man, a white man in a Hawaiian shirt.

"Mrs. Michaels? What's wrong? What's got you out so late?" he asked, like he didn't know already.

"It's Ava. She didn't come home."

Milford shook his head.

"Come on in," he said. His muscular arm reached out for me, and I allowed him to guide me to a chair in the small living room.

The white man came over and offered me a handkerchief.

"Thanks," I said, and got a good look at him. He was nearly bald with gray hair around the temples. He wasn't bad-looking, well built with kind eyes, but he had to be at least twenty years older than Milford.

"May I offer you something to drink?"

"Water, please." His deep voice took me by surprise. It wasn't at all sissified.

I thanked him, and drank the water quickly.

"Milford, do you know anything?"

Milford shrugged, and looked away from me.

"Lita, I promised Ava that I wouldn't tell you."

"You promised me, too, that you'd let me know what she was up to."

"That's true," Milford said and sat heavily on the couch. Even as big as he was, he still had a face of a boy.

Then the white man stepped up.

"I can help. By the way, my name is Chet Moore." He held his hand out. I shook it, and then he squatted down alongside of me.

"You know I teach at Dorsey. Milford keeps me up on all that goes on, and I think Milford wants for me to tell you where she is. That way he won't have to feel as though he's betrayed her."

"Okay," I said curtly. I was tired of these games, and I needed to get back to my kids.

"She's getting married."

My mouth fell open.

"That's impossible. She needs my permission."

"She said she had it. She left for Las Vegas."

I jumped up so fast I knocked the glass of water into the air as I rushed to the door.

"You can't catch them. They've been gone," Milford said.

"How could you let her go? She's a kid. What, she's seventeen, and she goes off and gets married!"

Milford shook his head like he had a headful of curls to shake back and forth.

"You don't know how she is. She's not a child. That girl is grown and does what she wants," Milford said, like he knew what he was talking about.

"Where is she staying in Vegas?"

Milford shook his head even more dramatically.

"I don't know."

I was about ready to fling the door open to leave when I stopped cold.

"Alright, who is this guy she's with?"

"His name is Earl. I only met him once. He's not what you think. He's not a bad guy. He's so religious. That's why he wants them to get married. He said that's the only way they could be together without sinning."

Now I was disgusted. Ava was born old with the kind of experience about life that I took forever to get. All my tricks, all my plotting to get out from underneath Mother, was nothing compared to how fast she got from underneath my control.

"How old is this Earl?"

Milford frowned before he spoke.

"He's nineteen."

"He's nineteen going on dead."

"Mrs. Michaels, don't talk like that. They're in love. It's beautiful."

"Oh, please, Milford. Don't get me started."

I turned and headed for the door, sick to my stomach with betrayal.

I hurried to the car, hoping to get home quickly. Then I heard a voice from behind me. I struggled to get the cleaver from my shoulder bag, turned with it in my hand ready to whack somebody. Milford! He stepped back, giving me a chance to calm my heart. Then he started talking quickly.

"Mrs. Michaels . . . Lita . . . I was wrong not to tell you. I should have but I, you know . . . I really want to be her friend. I tried to do the right thing."

I shrugged.

His long arm reached across the car and handed me a folded piece of paper.

It was the name of a casino in Vegas, the Moulin Rouge.

"Thank you," I said. "Now get in the car."

"What?" Milford look confused, but I set him straight.

"You're coming."

"Where're we supposed to be going?"

"Vegas."

Milford stood there, his arms wrapped around himself, deciding. Then he smiled like a kid who just discovered it was his birthday.

"I always wanted to go to Vegas!"

"Go put on your pants. It's a long drive."

Milford clapped his hands together and ran back for his clothes.

I was relieved to finally see Milford trotting to the car, carrying a grocery bag filled with clothes. Maybe I could set some of this nonsense right.

The lights were on in the kitchen, and I knew Winston was home. I hoped I could have slipped back into the house without having to explain anything to him.

Whenever that man made something to eat for himself, it sounded like World War II going on. He was at the sink hacking away at a ham bone, making a sandwich of gristle and cartilage.

This time he heard me sneaking by. Winston turned around, red-faced and scowling.

"Where were you?"

"It's Ava. She's run away."

Winston smirked.

"Really? That got you dragging around the street? What are you supposed to do about it? You got kids of your own to fret about."

I did my best to control my temper. Yes, I did, but this man was sorely tempting me.

"Did you hear me? I said that Ava run off to be married."

"Why should I complain about that? That's one less problem for us."

"How could you say some shit like that? She's just seventeen. You know that!"

"Good! She's gone. Who needs her?"

"Shut your mouth, Winston! That's my sister, and I'm going to find her. You need to watch our boys until I get back."

84

"Lita, you're staying right here!"

My first thought was to fling something at his head. He should have known better; hadn't we gone through this in the past? It was history, but it wasn't ancient; he had to know better. He had to know how it was. I looked around for something that was hard enough not to bounce off his thick skull. Then I saw Jude craning around the door. No, I wouldn't let myself see red. I could control myself, could calm myself. I turned around and headed to the bedroom for my overnight bag and my change jar, in case I had time for the slots. I walked to the front door, hoping that he wouldn't be stupid enough to try to stop me.

Soon as I put my hand on the knob I heard him.

"Lita! Stop! Don't you—"

That's when I flung that jar of pennies and nickels at him. Amazing how good that felt, seeing those coins spin and spill out as the mayonnaise jar arched toward Winston's head. It shattered against a wall, and he looked at me like I was as insane as a woman could be.

He was right.

*M*ilford *grinned at* me as I opened the car door.

"You ready for this? Ready for Vegas?"

I shrugged when I saw the porch light flick on and Winston come bursting out of the house.

"I'm ready to go," I said, and pulled out, seeing Winston, hands on hips, shrinking in the rearview mirror. Felt good, running out like that, leaving him behind in the dust.

Even hours later I was still giddy. Driving in the hot darkness of the 15 was tonic for me, washing away all that anger I had for letting myself become a woman I can't stand.

The wind blew in warm, but it dried the sweat dripping down my face. Milford snored loud in the backseat, his long frame stretched from end to end of the Galaxie 500.

I didn't need company, or the radio's static. I was content to dream of freedom, freedom of the right nickel, the nickel that would tell everybody where to go. Pull that handle and see those cherries line up, and for one beautiful moment I wouldn't need anyone or anything. That was my idea of heaven, a lucky Las Vegas heaven.

*T*wice we *stopped* for gas, and both times the attendant looked like he was ready to tell us to get the hell out of the station. Those white boys saw a white woman with a big black man and they knew what that meant, someone needed to be taught a lesson, but they'd be taught a lesson if they said a word in my direction.

Los Angeles taught me one thing; stare them in the eye, and make it clear that you will cause them more grief than they can cause you.

It worked. I got the gas, and we kept on; that's how it was going to be from now on.

Some twenty-five miles away, and I could see Vegas glowing like Christmas in the inky black of the desert night.

I called to Milford to wake up, to be amazed like I was the first time I saw it; it made me greedy for everything. Milford was still a boy, even if he looked like a man; he just muttered something about Mama and went right back to sleep.

Milford's crumpled piece of paper had in purple ink the name of the Moulin Rouge, far from Glitter Gulch, on the black side of town. I remember that casino; it was supposed to be nice. But after playing the slots there, I realized what was going on; since it was the casino for colored folk, you'd have to die and go to heaven before one of their slot machines paid off.

I found a parking space near the entrance of the casino, stepped out, and stretched my legs. I guess after

two babies and twenty-five pounds I shouldn't expect
to keep my looks, but from how that security guy ogled
me, I must still have something.

Milford still snored, but I needed to get started
looking for Ava.

I wondered if Winston was looking for me. Would
he actually drive out here and search for me like I
searched for my sister?

No, he needed to get to the post office and do his
shift. Winston wouldn't miss a day of precious employ-
ment even if I was being buried.

After nodding my thanks to the security guard for
making such a big deal of opening the door for me, I
stepped into the casino and all the brightness and noise,
halfway expecting to see Ava there waiting on me with
her new husband. I imagined me a flaming madwoman,
pulling that girl down and whupping her ass black and
blue.

No, just a mess of people milling around, dropping
coins into the one-armed jacks, but not Ava and her
statutory rapist husband.

All that sound of coins rattling down, the screams of
happiness, was surely tempting, but I knew I had to at
least look for Ava and her husband. I forgot that little
shit's name. I unfolded the paper again. The name read
"Earl Duplaix." God, another asshole with a French
name. Might as well been back in New Orleans chasing
after Adele. I shouldn't be pretending that this wasn't
what it was, life-and-death serious, another fool sister

chasing love straight to the grave. Mother was right; we Du Champs are cursed. Our family's tragedy didn't start with Adele, and it won't end with her, if Ava doesn't watch it. Blind love kills us; men like Lucien are everywhere. That's why I married Winston; I might have made a stupid mistake, but Winston had reason to fear for his life from me, not the other way around.

88

The slots lost their allure; the casino became a shoe box of annoying noise and gaudy, tacky bullshit. I found the hotel clerk shuffling papers behind the counter.

The clerk didn't want to be helpful, with his askew tie and silly cowlick. This was supposed to be a colored hotel, but still they let white folks work. In New Orleans we had sense to do to whites what they did to us.

"We don't give out that information," he said, looking at me like I was in the wrong place.

"Listen," I said, "I'm trying to find my sister. She's underage and is with a man who needs to be arrested."

He raised an eyebrow.

"That's right. So I would appreciate you taking a look at your book and telling me where they are."

This little ofay still thought he could blow me off. I gritted my teeth and tried to keep from hopping that counter and beating some politeness into him.

"Don't make me mad. You don't want me to get mad, no," I said, gripping the edge of the counter so hard my knuckles went bloodless and numb.

"Here you go, lady," he said, and I could see the fear in him, in his eyes.

That made me feel good.

I walked back into the hot night and found the car and opened the back door.

Milford's big head fell back, and he sat up in a panic.

"What the hell is going on!" he shouted.

"Milford, I got the room number."

He took a second to collect himself.

"Look, maybe you ought to change into long pants," I said, looking at his muscular dark legs.

"Why? It's hot."

"I know it's hot, but you're underage, and you're going into a casino."

"Yeah?"

I rolled my eyes.

"I need you. If this fool doesn't listen to reason, some very bad things might happen."

"I got that. I can handle that."

"And if you're going to crack somebody's head, you need to be in long pants."

Milford took a second to think about it, then turned to me and nodded.

"I get your point."

Shrugging, Milford opened the paper bag with his change of clothes, shut the car door, and slipped into long pants.

Inside the casino, near the hotel room Ava was supposedly honeymooning in, I gave Milford his instructions.

"I'm going to knock on the door, and when Ava opens it, I'm going to pull her out and talk some sense to her. You don't have to do a thing, unless that play husband of hers gets out of hand."

I took a minute to collect myself, then knocked hard at the door. I knocked again and heard footsteps approach. The door swung open, and I saw this little man in a smoking jacket. I almost wanted to laugh. He was handsome, but so damn short that he probably needed a phone book to reach her lips.

"Where's Ava?"

"Who are you?" he asked.

"I'm her sister."

"But that don't give you the right to come barging in here."

He puffed up his chest, trying to impress me. That boy was so slight, I couldn't imagine how he could get around Ava's boobs to hold her. For the life of me I couldn't imagine what she saw in a man that made Winston look tall.

"Listen, lady, I don't care who you are, you getting out of this room!"

That's when I lost my temper and shoved him aside.

"Ava, where the hell are you?"

I looked around the hotel room and the closet. I

checked under the bed and saw a pair of red pumps. That cheeky little bitch! Those were my pumps.

As I picked up the shoes, somebody shoved me hard in the back. I landed on the bed and looked up to see that boy trying to manhandle me.

"You must be joking!" I said, and hauled off and kneed him where it counts.

The little pervert moaned, and for good measure I took one of those red pumps that Ava thought she should use without even asking me and hit him square on the head. Then I gave him an elbow to the stomach, and he dropped to his knees.

"Don't get up, because I will break your behind. I promise you that."

When he didn't say anything, I hit him in the head with the shoe again to make sure he was listening.

Ava had to be hiding in the bathroom.

"Ava, open the damn door before I get Milford to knock it down."

Still nothing.

"Tell you what. I'm gonna go call Milford in here and tell him to carry this little runt of a so-called man down to the hotel clerk and have him call the police. You might not know this, but he committed a crime marrying you, and I sure as hell wouldn't mind seeing him go to jail."

"Lita," I heard from the other side of the door.

"Don't Lita me, just open this shitting door and come home with me."

More silence.

"Don't be making me wait. You don't have a choice."

The door creaked open, and I saw her standing there in a bright red slip, her face all made up like a baboon's ass and her breasts looking like two gigantic overripe tomatoes about to burst.

She must have damn near broke that little boy's back.

"Okay, Ava, you're done playing house. You're coming home, and don't start with any of that I'm-grown bullshit."

"Lita, you've got no right doing this. You're not Mother."

I slapped Ava one good one for all the trouble she caused, and because I needed to. I didn't want to talk to her. I wanted to talk to this little squid that thought he could rob the cradle and not have a price to pay. Yeah, I wanted to talk to this one, set him straight. Read him the riot act, how damn sure serious I was.

I couldn't at first; I had to catch my breath, calm myself. What I felt, this blind rage, scared me.

I turned to Earl and lifted my shoe just to see him flinch. He was a lot more afraid of me than of Milford. "I'm going to tell you this once, and once only. Come around my family again, and I will kill you. Don't doubt me, no. If I don't do it with my own hands, I will pay someone to do it. I know about people like you, using women, and when you don't get your way, you kick them on their asses. Sometimes you kill them. I know how you men are."

The boy looked at me with pleading eyes, like he had enough courage to state his case, then he realized how close he was to something painful happening to him, and he looked down at the floor, defeated.

I wasn't angry anymore. It had escaped like air from a balloon. I just wanted to go into the bathroom and throw up.

"Lita, you're wrong," Ava said. She had a robe on now, tears rolling down from her eyes; the thick makeup streaked from it.

I thought about it, but I couldn't remember ever seeing Ava cry.

"How am I wrong? If somebody is wrong, it's you. When does a seventeen-year-old get to go off to Vegas to get married? What gives you the right? Why is it right that I get the burden of raising you! What kind of life have I had? What about me?"

Ava stared at me with her beautiful tear-stained eyes and changed me around, made me feel like a fool.

"That's right, Lita. You right. That's why I don't want to live like you. I want my own life now, not when you say so."

I shook my head. She wasn't going to give up what she thought she had, freedom.

"Well, that's too bad," I said, straight-faced, when

inside I was collapsing. I had nothing else inside of me to draw upon. No more anger, just fatigue.

Ava walked around me and slipped her arms around that little undeserving boy, administering to where I had clocked him on the head.

"Lita, you know I'm not a child. You know what I went through, what we all went through in New Orleans. How can you expect me to want to play with dolls and make silly with girls who don't know a thing? Earl, he's in the army. He wants me to go with him to Georgia. That's why we got married. He wanted me to be his wife, and I wanted to be his wife. I can't wait for a couple more years, pretending I'm happy living here with you."

I shook my head and laughed like she was all wrong. Oh, she didn't know. I wanted her to go as much as she wanted to go, to be free of her, of my family. Oh, yes, that was what I wanted, but Ava didn't know what guilt was, didn't know how Mother could make you feel like the whole world rested on whether or not you could change somebody's diaper in two seconds and get back to the bar to serve drunks more cheap-ass beer. Already I was drowning in a river of guilt, just thinking about how much I wanted to tell Ava to just leap in headfirst and start her life as a woman. See what that's like, all the laughs and the happiness she'll share when the first child is born and the grind sets in; of working, of being a wife. At least in her case she won't have the pleasure of having to raise a little sister like herself.

Earl looked at me from the corner of his eye, like he had something to say.

"Look, miss, I didn't mean to get on your bad side, but I really do love Ava."

"Did I say you could talk to me?"

The boy averted his eyes.

"What do you know about love?" I asked him.

"I know I'm in love with her. I never loved anybody like I love her," he said, solemnly.

"You religious?" I asked.

"Oh, yes. I go to the God in Christ on Adams."

"No, we're Catholics. You respect that!"

"I respect that."

I looked at him. The poor boy; he had no idea of what he was up against. My God, Ava was going to eat him alive; wouldn't even be any bones left.

"If you so God-fearing, why didn't you talk to me, see what I had to say, being that I'm Ava's guardian?"

"Ava," he said, darting his eyes in her direction.

"Ava?" I said, glancing at my devious little sister, and I saw that brief smirk flit across her face.

Should have figured.

"This is your doing?" I asked.

Ava didn't bother being coy. She knew that wouldn't save her.

"Lita, why you pretending you would have even listened to me? You wouldn't have let me go."

I counted to ten. I had already slapped her, and I didn't want to make it any more of a habit.

"No, I wouldn't have let you go. Mother wouldn't have wanted me to do that. She would have wanted me to keep you doing the right thing. What you've done is wrong, and Mother would have beaten you black and blue to set you straight."

"But you're not Mother," Ava said under her breath.

96

"What's that you said?"

Ava covered her face with her hands.

"I'm not going to be hitting you. You're grown. You want to be on your own, be on your own."

She looked at me suspiciously.

"You don't mean that."

"You want a trial marriage?"

She looked at me with a open face, not with anger or scorn.

"You would do that?"

"Yeah."

I turned to Earl and gave him my most evil look.

"I'm gonna tell you this once. If this girl comes running back to me with a black eye, a broken rib, or a chipped tooth, you are dead. Do you understand me?"

Earl nodded.

I stood up and handed Ava my red pumps. I didn't need them. Winston didn't dance, and now, neither did I.

"That's your wedding present," I said to her. Ava looked at me with big watery eyes.

Like some monster sleeping at the bottom of the

ocean, the love I felt for this beautiful sister of mine surfaced.

I held her tightly and whispered, "I love you, Ava."

"I love you too, Lita."

I turned for the door and remembered Milford, stretched out on the bed, watching us like his own private soap opera.

"Come on, maybe we can play some slots before we head back."

As I shut the door, I saw them embracing; that little man smothered in Ava's cleavage.

*W*e *played twenty* dollars' worth of slots before we got back on the road. Again, I was driving because Milford didn't have a license and the highway patrol would have loved to pull over a black man and when they saw me there would be no end of trouble. He was in the backseat, asleep again. I was glad for that; all he could talk about the first hour of the drive was how beautiful Ava looked. It was amazing, even sissies got hot for her.

The hot night air suited me; it seemed a bit cooler, but it wasn't that — I finally had got loose from the big rock of responsibility Mother had tied around my neck. Yes, I was free, swimming to the surface, ready to break through the water and fill my lungs with fresh air. Ready and eager to live my life.

I wanted to believe that, that things would go my way, but the truth was much more bitter and complicated. I wouldn't be free of New Orleans that easily; Mother's will was stronger than I imagined.

Happiness.

That notion escaped me. Ava could believe in happiness because she didn't know any better; time hadn't succeeded in beating it out of her.

After dropping off Milford, I came home so tired I wove through early-morning traffic like a drunk, the rising sun a blinding ball in my rearview mirror. Grateful to arrive back in one piece, I hurried to the porch, squinting in the harshness of the morning light.

Winston was at work, but I still felt nervous sneaking into the house, as if Mother was waiting on me with a switch in hand, ready to beat her rules into my behind. Little Winston and Jude were still in bed, so I had to shout for them to get the hell up and dressed, and of course I had to go into the bedroom and open the curtains and slide the pillows from beneath their heads.

"Get up! I don't want to have those nuns on my back!"

My oldest had problems with some of the nuns at Holy Name who were driving me crazy with their silly calls. They always had something bad to say: that Winston wasn't working hard enough at being an altar boy, he slept in class, he didn't want to do more than throw a football. The worst was said about my baby, Jude; that he didn't know what he should know, that he was behind for the first grade. Jesus! Wasn't that their job, to teach him?

I decided to keep Jude home from school when I saw the bags under his eyes.

He must have hardly slept after I left for Vegas, and Winston must have fed the boy all kinds of vicious shit about what I was up to. He was so surprised and happy to see me, jumping up into my arms like I had been gone for weeks, it confirmed my suspicions that Winston had told him I wouldn't be coming back, or some other nonsense. I was about to fix him breakfast when he tugged at my arm.

"Mama, Daddy didn't go to work," he said, and I heard the door open behind me. My jaw dropped; Winston stepped into the kitchen looking at me with complete contempt.

He was wearing his oil-stained jumpsuit with a wrench in hand. Men and their damn uniforms; Winston wouldn't have felt dressed without some tool clutched in his hand.

"What are you doing home?" I asked. He seemed surprised, as though he was the one who should be asking the questions. I got the jump on him; let him know I wasn't in the mood to be messed with.

"Okay, what was that all about? Running off, leaving me with the boys while you go galavanting."

Jude glanced up from his breakfast cereal, frowning like he knew he'd be ringside to another one of our knockdown, dropkick fights. I felt bad that the boy had to be in the middle, but I wasn't going to take any shit from Winston.

"Listen, Winston, I had family business and you know that. I did what I had to do."

I had the refrigerator open, reaching in for something to cook. I pulled free from the clutter of bags of frozen peas and corn a ten-pound ham, when I heard Winston's insult.

"So did you find the little slut?"

I lifted the frozen cylinder of meat over my head and flung it, twirling end over end, at Winston's head, but then it fell sharply, straight for Jude. For a moment I thought I was going to brain my boy.

Thank God, it missed and landed on his bowl of cereal, shattering it in his face. Winston jumped backward, stunned. Then he covered his head, worried that I might grab something else and try again.

"That's it, Lita. That's the last straw," Winston said, and grabbed for Jude's hand. "Let's get some breakfast."

"Listen, while you're out getting pancakes, look for a damn apartment," I shouted, to give Winston something else to chew on.

*W*inston and *I* had to go our separate ways, but was I ready to be a single mother of two boys? Did I have a choice?

Watching Winston walk back and forth from the garage to the house, tracking oil over the carpets even after I paid to have them shampooed, had me boiling mad. Mad enough that I knew it wasn't healthy or right for me to be that bent out of shape over him doing the same things he'd been doing since we were married. Sooner or later I would hit him in the head with a frozen turkey or a pot roast, and end up in jail for manslaughter. Just listening to him breathing was provocation enough to get me searching through the freezer for ammunition, but since he started working the morning shift, we got to hear him trumpet revelry with his hands. Waking up to something like that is . . .

Mental cruelty.

I heard about that at work. This old blond broad who was divorcing her husband of twenty years bragged to everybody about how her lawyer had it pegged, that her husband was guilty of mental cruelty. When somebody asked her how so, all this woman could do was shrug and say something about his attitude.

That got me to thinking—if anybody was mentally cruel, it had to be Winston.

I couldn't get him to listen to me about anything, but now he would have to listen to me, or to my lawyer.

Somebody asked me, what about the children? You got to think about the children.

I was thinking about them. If they wanted a living father and not a dead one, I needed to get this man out of my hair.

102

Lawyers don't come cheap, but I found one who would work for change under the couch, or so I was told by my coworker. I should have known what I was getting into; cheap is usually trash. The office waiting room smelled of cigarettes and spilled liquor. I could barely stand it; why the hell were the windows shut on a warm day? I sat on a hard chair until this bouffant-wigged woman stuck her head around the door to his inner office and waved for me.

I walked in and got a look at this lawyer. God, he was one tub of lard. The chair he sat in was as big around as a barrel, but he flowed like melting ice cream out of its confines.

He didn't bother to stand to shake my hand; he just seemed to breathe harder, like that was greeting enough. After lighting a cigarette and inhaling deeply, he smiled. I tried not to laugh, looking at this Sydney Greenstreet-looking black man.

"Lita Michaels," I said, after a long, awkward silence.

"Bob Cooney, attorney-at-law, at your service," he said.

"Pleased to meet you," I replied, trying to breathe out of my mouth, suspecting that this man must bathe only for major holidays.

"We talked on the phone earlier today?"

"Yes," I said, more sure with each passing second that this was a bad idea, and I needed to run for it.

"You're seeking a divorce, correct?"

I nodded.

He gestured to a sad little folding chair that someone had used to hold a ashtray, more ashes on the chair than in the tray. I moved the ashtray and wiped the chair with tissue, but there was no reason for me to be there; I had already made up my mind to put the divorce off until I could save up enough money to hire a lawyer who wasn't disgusting. He reached for the pack of cigarettes on the desk, pulled one out, and handed it to me.

"You smoke?"

I took the cigarette, and he deftly lit it for me. And there I was, nervously puffing and even inhaling, and to my surprise I didn't choke. I guess being around smokers all my life prepared me for it.

"Yes, I need a divorce, but my husband would never agree to it."

"Oh, don't you worry. In California we have laws that enable you to pursue divorce without your husband's consent; that is, if you have irreconcilable differences."

"Irreconcilable differences?"

"Yes, that's when you can't under any circumstances live under one roof. Did you catch him with another woman?"

"No."

"Does he gamble or steal?"

"No."

"He drinks?"

"Milk."

"Who are you married to, a bloody plaster saint?"

I shrugged. "Yes, I am."

"Does he beat you?"

For a moment I sat there, trying to think of how to reply to that. If anything, I was the one who did the beating, or at least the throwing.

"No."

"He really is some kind of saint," the lawyer said, shaking his fat head.

"What about mental cruelty?"

"I was just getting ready to mention that. That's a big one," he said, smirking.

"Aren't you going to ask me how he is mentally cruel?"

"No, but I'll get my secretary to type something up."

"Good," I said. "How much is this going to cost me?"

He blinked his eyes at me like some damn turtle. Didn't I read somewhere that if someone blinks when they're telling you something, they're lying, or getting ready to lie?

"I'll get you a price that'll be competitive."

"What the hell does that mean?"

"Nobody is going to charge you less."

"Well, how much are you charging?"

"That depends."

"Suppose I tell you that I got seventy-five dollars."

He laughed, trying to hide his mouth with one of his sausagelike hands.

"You know how weddings are. Divorces are like that. Cheap may be nice in its own way, but you can't expect champagne and caviar."

"I never had caviar, and champagne makes me throw up."

"Well!" he said. "How about that."

He paused to thumb through a pile of documents and then turned back to me.

"Let's say three hundred. For three hundred you'll get the house, and for five hundred your kids get as much child support as we can squeeze out of your soon-to-be-broke ex-husband."

"That's pretty steep for me."

He laughed, snorting.

"It might seem steep, but you know these things get complicated. Billable hours need to be paid. I wish I could work for free, but a man's got to eat, put food on the table, see to the needs of his children."

"How soon can you get started?"

"Now! I can get the paperwork done by tomorrow, file it, and get a court date."

"That's it?" I asked. It almost seemed too easy, but a

chill ran through me. I even started to shake; if this is what I wanted, why did I feel so bad?

I stood up abruptly.

"Wait a minute, lady. We can work something out. How about four hundred dollars for the full divorce?"

I ignored him as I walked quickly to the door.

6

Time passed, and New Orleans lost its hold on my boys. Los Angeles became their home, and they accepted that; lemon trees replaced banana trees, Volkswagen Bugs replaced dragonflies and flying cockroaches. Big Winston didn't seem to miss New Orleans at all, and me, I didn't know what to think.

At times I wanted to return home, but I liked the cool nights even in the hottest months of the summer; cool nights were something you could only pray for in New Orleans. After hell broke out in Los Angeles, I did consider returning. I had taken the kids to Griffin Park to the observatory. We were having a good time dropping pennies into the telescope and looking about the city. When I glanced to the east, I saw black smoke coming up. I didn't know then what was happening, but

I did as soon as I turned the radio on. The Watts riots had started. We drove down into erupting mayhem; the fires were still distant, but we tasted their acrid sting. Grim-faced National Guard troops drove down Exposition in jeeps with fifty-caliber machine guns mounted onto them. We even saw tanks in the streets, waiting for what, I don't know. That's when I started to think that going back to New Orleans might be a good thing.

Winston acted like at any moment crazy black people would kick down our door, toss a Molotov cocktail into our living room, and kill us all. I tried to calm him, but it was hopeless; he insisted on keeping the boys in the back room, huddled together on the far corner of the bed, waiting for the worst to happen. They couldn't help but be scared when their father insisted on patrolling the house with a shotgun resting on his shoulder.

"Winston, put that shotgun down. The National Guard is out there on the street. It's curfew. You can't drive nowhere or be on the streets. Stop worrying."

Winston grunted and continued marching around the house, checking and rechecking doors, locks, and windows, peering through curtains and the peephole for trouble, carrying that shotgun on his shoulder like it was a Veterans Day parade. Finally, he wore down and collapsed into a chair. When he thought I wasn't looking, his eyes shut with that shotgun resting across his lap like a TV dinner tray. I slipped it from his hands, unloaded the shells, and locked it in the hall closet.

I was done.

The city could burn down, but I didn't give a damn; I had my own fires to put out.

I *finally had* the money for a real attorney, Steve Goldberg, and I wanted the divorce finalized as quickly as possible, but the riots shot all that to hell.

Sometimes I could do it, make myself so angry, pissed off, that nothing could scare me, but the riots were something else. Now, getting mistaken for white could mean being dragged from a car and beaten by a mob, even raped or killed. I felt relief when I saw the police manning checkpoints, but I knew I was in for a big hassle. They wouldn't even pretend to listen to what I had to say. To them I was a white woman trying to get around the barricades into Niggerville.

Winston took the divorce like a baby, making a big scene on the porch in front of the children, like I was sending him away to die.

I didn't tell him to get an apartment on Fifty-fourth Street and Slausion, pretty close to where the fires were raging. He shouldn't have been so damn cheap, but it wasn't that he was just cheap. It was another one of his dumb games, picking a dump to move into because he thought I'd soon get over wanting the divorce. As though me being sick of him was the result of having my mind poisoned by an extra-long period, and when it ended I'd be back to putting up with him. Sometimes in the middle of an argument he'd say, Lita, your waters are roiling. He was right about that; my waters were roiling, and they wouldn't ever calm as long as he was in my life.

Winston was gone, washed right out of my hair. I had what I wanted—to be on my own, taking care of myself and my kids like I had been doing most of my life. Now I wouldn't be answering to anybody but me. It would have been perfect, except that Winston wasn't ready to let it go. He couldn't accept what was the most obvious thing; I was free of him. He'd call and plead his case, that he'd change, though he didn't know what he did that was so bad. That we could work it out and it was best for the kids and certainly the best thing for my reputation. That's when I would hang up on him. Then he started getting slick on me, calling our mutual friends, Thelma and Norman, friends that we had from New Orleans who had headed out to California and stuck together like the Creole Mafia. Winston probably thought that would carry weight with me, that the loud-ass card games we would play with these Creoles meant something to me. I hated it and them, screaming at some half-deaf, drunk, and bellicose fool who would stab you with the Vienna sausage fork over twenty-five cents that they thought they were owed. Oh, no. I had enough of that shit to last me a lifetime. Winston could take his Creole friends and his Creole world. Soon as I heard, "Hey, Lita, this is Thelma, Winston asked me to—"

"Thelma, you listen to this. I'm through with Winston. Mind your own damn business."

His friends kept calling, and I kept giving them shit until they too were out of my hair.

Winston was free to come by and take the kids anytime he wanted. I didn't have a problem with him being with his kids. I would never deny him that.

But the shit he'd pull! Sometimes I felt like loading everything into the car and heading for the hills.

I was in the middle of getting dinner ready, rushing because I had to do the evening shift at work, when I heard the doorbell ring. I decided to let Jude deal with it. I had just got a pot of hot water on for noodles when he came into the kitchen, looking sheepish.

"What's wrong, honey?"

"There's a priest at the door."

"A priest?"

"Father Brown."

"Oh, Jesus! You tell that priest that I don't want to talk to him."

Jude lingered in the kitchen, staring at his shoes.

"Go ahead," I said, and turned him around and sent him back to the priest.

I sucked air, cursing Winston. That bastard! I told him not to send somebody over from the church to get me to change my mind.

I slipped into a chair and forced back tears. What the hell would a priest have to say to me that would make any difference? What did they know, anyway? Being married to the church had to be a lot easier than being married to Winston. The church didn't throw the jelly of a jelly doughnut away, talking about you don't need it.

Jude stuck his head into the kitchen, "He won't go."

"What do you mean he won't go?"

"He says he's gonna wait until you're finished with dinner."

"Shit!" I threw down a potholder and headed for the front door.

I didn't know this Father Brown, but I heard he had a way with the ladies. Someone had mentioned there was a new priest, and since Winston seemed to live at the damn church, crying on the shoulder of anybody in the rectory, it figured he'd have Father Brown's ear.

Father Brown was new all right, young, tall, well built, and blond. I could see why the church hens were all hot and bothered.

He stuck his hand out, but I ignored it.

"Hello, Lita. Please excuse me for dropping by unannounced, but I thought maybe we could talk for a moment."

I gritted my teeth, doing my best not to curse this priest.

"Father, I'm busy at the moment, trying to get dinner on the table before work."

"Lita, this is important, and I can promise you it'll only take a few minutes."

Father Brown reached for my hand, gave me a reassuring pat, and stepped into the house.

I sighed.

It didn't end; Winston would do anything in his power to keep it from ending.

"Your husband asked me to speak to you."

"You mean my ex-husband."

"Yes, well, that's why I wanted to talk to you. I've been counseling him on the issues of conflict in your marriage."

I bit my lip.

"Father, there isn't any relationship, so there's no conflict."

"Lita, in the eyes of the Lord, your relationship still stands."

I sighed again, rubbing my hands together, imagining what it would be like to have my hands around Winston's neck.

"Your husband still loves you."

I couldn't help it; I still had respect for the church, but at this point, I don't know why, words came spilling out of my mouth.

"Father, I don't care if he loves me, I'm not going to live with him. It's that simple."

He looked at me with such caring eyes. I had to

admit he was good-looking, and the way his hand rested on mine . . . For a moment I was open to hearing what he had to say.

"Lita, you have a clear and obvious choice: either you can choose the path of reconciliation with Winston and the church, or you can choose the path of divorce and excommunication. By severing your relationship with your husband, you also sever your relationship with the church. You'll be adrift, without the grace of Jesus to make eternal life possible."

"In other words, if I don't remarry Winston, I'm going to die and go to hell?"

"It's not as simple as that."

"But that's what I'm hearing."

"Lita, you need to think about your children, you need to think about your reputation. You need to think about that man that you left shattered, unable to put his life back together."

Oh, he was laying it on thick, bringing out the evil in me.

"I guess love don't count."

"Love counts, but what we're talking about is more important than love; obedience, acceptance, and submission."

"I guess you don't know much about love, Father. I want love in my life. Not love of being ground down by a man. Winston isn't a bad man. I admit he's a good one—doesn't drink, doesn't try to hit me, brings his money home every week. But that's not enough."

I could tell from Father Brown's expression he didn't like how the conversation was going.

"See, Father, my life has been about doing for others, doing for my sisters, for my mother, my kids, Winston, but never for me. It's never been about me. I don't need a man in my life because I need him to support me. I rely on myself. I need a man in my life because I love him and I want him there."

115

Father Brown shook his head.

"Lita, that's not the answer. That's not acknowledging the word of God and the sanctity of marriage."

I took my time replying. I felt like a cat with a mouse between its paws.

"Father, I know you're not married, but I'm sure you've had your share of relationships."

Father Brown stepped back, an awkward smile stuck on his face. He must know we all talk. What else are we going to do but talk about what our priests are up to? There was enough gossip about Father Brown. Bet my last dollar that there's scandal behind his name.

"Lita, I'm not the subject at hand. You are the one that needs to consider your relationship with your husband."

"Ex!" I shouted.

Father Brown looked like he had enough of me and started backing up to the door.

"Lita, let me be blunt. If you make the wrong decision, if you leave your marriage and turn your back on the church, then the church will have no alternative but to excommunicate you."

I laughed right in his face.

"So, even though I'm doing what's right for me, trying to start over and build a life for myself, the church is going to turn its back on me?"

"Lita, excommunication is not something the church chooses to do lightly, but you leave no choice."

"Oh, please! You have a choice. Get off my property before I do something I regret."

Even though he had given me reason, I can't say I wanted the reputation of breaking a broom over a priest's head.

"You should consider what I said when you're not so emotional."

I had to smile at him.

"Sure, I'll think about it."

His time was up with me, but he had sense enough to go before I found the broom.

Part Two

7

*A*unt Dot called, and I heard her words, but they didn't mean a thing to me. I didn't have much to keep me in Los Angeles, but returning to New Orleans still seemed out of the question. I did my best to put her nonsense out of my mind. With Mother long dead, I had no reason to return, certainly not to help Daddy make amends for all the wrong he did in life.

Then I felt Mother's presence, smelled her perfume. I sat up in bed and called out for her. I was a child again, waiting for her to come see about me.

It felt good and right. Everything would be made better if she would just come through that door and pick me up in her arms.

I waited, but she didn't come.

The child withered away, and the adult was left

there, hoping for a miracle, a miracle that passed me by.

Still, I longed to see her; to see her face would be enough.

Nothing, just a long moment of anticipation, resulting in me sitting there rigid as steel until I broke down and fell back to sleep.

But sleep and wakefulness were the same for me. I tried to conjure her again, but no, I couldn't imagine her face.

I felt it; Mother was unhappy with me.

Daddy?

Was I supposed to return to New Orleans to see him, after all that louse of a man did to the family?

If that was true, then I needed a concrete sign, a sign that could make me suspend whatever common sense I had to waste time and money on a trip home.

I told myself that I didn't believe in signs, didn't want visitations; everything would be revealed soon enough in the next life.

It bothered me that anyone and their grandmother seemed to have had one from Mother except for me.

Now I had mine.

Mother came to me. It wasn't a coincidence; it couldn't be a damn coincidence.

No, whatever mess I made of life in Los Angeles, I still couldn't go back with my tail between my legs.

However lonely and worn ragged I might feel, I had made my bed in Los Angeles, and I had to sleep in it.

But Mother came to me because she wanted me home.

For what?

To see about Ava or Ana, or maybe it's Richie or, I'll never understand it, Daddy.

That's how Mother would do it. Give me a mission, something I could pursue like a stupid dog right off the nearest cliff.

That's what I've always done: raise my sisters, run the bar, deal with Daddy, then Adele, then Lucien.

It's what Mother wanted me to do.

I don't know if she loved me like a child, or like a tool, something she needed to shovel all the shit of the Du Champ family with.

She loved me like a damned shovel.

*P*lans exploded into bits, especially if they had anything to do with my ex-husband. I never thought it would be so much trouble to get a man to take his own son for a few weeks, but no, Winston had his own ideas about what I should or couldn't do.

My oldest boy already lives with him. Little Winston is always in and out of trouble, and I thought I'd let his Daddy try his hand at raising that boy. Jude, my youngest, lives with me. He's sweet, but he has bad nerves, and I worry for him. His father says I need to let him grow up; I tell him to mind his own business. I wish I had someone who could have kept me from growing up for a little while longer. If I can give Jude something I didn't have—a childhood—things might go right for him, more right than they ever went for me.

I had to explain slowly and carefully exactly what the facts were. That we were not married and that the kids were still his and that I needed him to act like a goddamned father to both his children.

"My apartment is too small for two boys. Take him with you."

I knew what the bastard was up to.

"Why should I take Jude? My father is dying, a man he doesn't know, and I don't want him to know. He'll miss school for a funeral that will mean nothing to him."

"Because you should."

"No, Winston, it's because you think I'm going down there to meet some man."

Winston snickered, and I slapped him hard on the face.

"Don't make fun of me, Winston."

His hand darted up, and he slapped me, too.

This is where I stepped back and assessed the situation. There we were out in the middle of the street, neighbors laughing, watching us exchange slaps.

I rubbed my cheek and inhaled deeply.

"I'll let that pass, Winston."

"You started it. You're the one who hauled off and hit me in the kisser."

"You deserved it! Implying what the hell you were implying!"

He shook his head like he was pitying me. I had to take two deep breaths not to slap him again.

"Take the boy, or you will never see him again," I said.

"You have to! The judge said—"

"The judge can go to hell. I have a family emergency, and if you can't take him for two weeks, you don't ever need to take him."

I was serious about it too. Dead serious, and if he thought I was joking, he'd spend the rest of his life trying to remember what his son even looked like.

That was it. He folded his arms around himself and watched me walk back into the house.

Another battle done with so I could return somewhere I didn't want to go. It didn't make sense, but neither did my life.

*R*iding *across five* states in a Greyhound bus isn't as bad as driving across those same states pregnant with hot wind blowing in your face, your husband whistling "America the Beautiful" for five hundred miles and nowhere to lay your head because the car is cluttered with crap and kids, but it comes close.

I didn't mind that many of the people who sat next

to me didn't speak a word of English, but they seemed surprised and irritated that I didn't speak a word of Spanish.

Then the cowboys. My God, I didn't think cowboys caught the Greyhound, but they do; colored ones, Mexican ones, white ones, with dirty jeans, Stetsons, worn-down boots. And none of them know how to bathe. I just clutched my purse and held on to my letter opener and one unopened letter. Sit with a sharp instrument, and even stupid people get the idea that you don't want to be pawed, unless, that is, they want to paw you with one less finger or maybe with a six-inch blade in their thigh.

I'm almost embarrassed to admit how happy I was when the bus finished the drive through the deserts from Arizona to west Texas. When we neared Houston and things greened up and you could hear the cicadas and see creeks along the highway, I felt relief, a relief I was surprised to feel. I didn't know I'd feel anything but unease, returning to the wet heat and decay of New Orleans.

Almost home, but some home to go home to.

We pulled into the Greyhound terminal, and my relief evaporated. A residue of fear was left in its place, bitter and dry in my mouth.

I didn't want Ana to see me before I got to clean up. I looked like hell, smelled like a Greyhound honeypot, and felt like shit.

I dragged my suitcase into the restroom that wasn't much cleaner than the one on the bus, though it was bigger. I could slip into a stall and change into a clean dress. I brushed my teeth and did something with my hair. I wouldn't say I looked presentable, but it was the best I could do under the circumstances; I was doing everything with one hand, while the other still held on to the letter opener. Changing shoes was truly a circus tightrope walk, juggling everything while trying not to step on the pee-stained floor with a bare foot.

Finally, I was ready to meet my sister.

Crowded and loud, the Greyhound depot seemed more like a Mardi Gras party than anything else. I could barely see six feet in front of me, let alone find Ana. Ready to give up, I headed to the exits, looking for a taxi because my backside couldn't stand another bus.

I saw Ana at the telephones, twisting the phone cord in her hands, worry on her face, but at the same time she looked gorgeous in an expensive and prim dress. She was a redhead now, which made her pale skin look even paler. Bet she got dolled up for me, just to make me feel even more like shit.

"Ana!" I called to her.

She rushed to me and wrapped her arms around my neck and squeezed like she actually missed me.

"Lita, I'm glad you're home!"

She stood back to look me over.

"You look great! You held up on the ride just fine. I

don't do so good on the bus. I told George when we visit New York again we were flying, and that's what we did."

"You look beautiful, Ana, and your dress is beautiful too."

I wanted to ask where she got the pattern from, but then I realized she probably didn't sew.

"How's the family?" she asked.

"The boys are staying with Winston."

"How is Winston? I heard you were having problems."

I laughed as I struggled with my suitcase to the exit.

Luckily, Ana's car was parked close to the bus terminal. I only strained my back a little bit.

"You two on the rocks?"

I snorted.

"Ana, we've been divorced for the last four years."

Ana exhaled. How could she be shocked? Sure, we didn't talk much. I didn't know it was that bad, but it was. Hell, I didn't go to her wedding, didn't know the names of her kids.

I was truly an exile in California.

But Ava and Ana were obviously comfortable with the idea. I guess it was to be expected that with everything that happened it would take a decade to pass before we could stand to see each other.

"It must be difficult. How do you handle all that? Working, raising the kids, paying the mortgage."

"Listen, I did a lot of that when I was married to the man."

Obviously Ana didn't work, happy at home.

"There's child support. He pays that. You learn to make ends meet. It's not that big a deal."

Ana eased her well-maintained Cadillac into traffic. She wasn't a particularly good driver, but she didn't make me want to leap out of the car.

127

"George is good to me. He's a great provider," Ana said, innocently enough. It wasn't like she was rubbing in the fact that I had no provider except for myself. "I'm in school now. Two more years and I'll have my bachelor's."

"That's great," I said. "I'm happy for you."

Lying through my teeth. How the hell did she have it so made? Didn't she have kids—three?

"Ana, I know this is going to sound silly, but I forgot how many kids you have."

"Four. The youngest, Henry, is two years."

"That's wonderful. It's amazing how much you get done, raising a big family and all."

"That's George for you. He works extra hard so we can have someone come in."

"Come in?"

"To watch the kids, keep the house. Most of the times I cook, but George does like to barbeque."

I had to shake my head. My sister was living the life.

"You got it made, sugar," I said, trying to conceal the jealousy dripping from my lips.

She pulled into the driveway of a pretty home on a street of new homes, ranch-style, like you see in Los Angeles.

Ana smiled as the front door opened and her kids came bursting outside to greet us.

"I admit it, I'm spoiled," she said.

At least she admits it. It almost makes it okay, almost.

I met George. As I figured, he was older, maybe in his late thirties, a lucky man with a attractive wife in her early twenties. He had the kind of job that folks dream about. Ana said with pride that he was the new dean of students at Xavier. So that explained the easy life and Ava's college education to boot. What a catch! The man seemed nice enough—brown-skinned, tall, a little on the thin side, and going gray early. He was good with the kids. Just off work, he got down on the rug with the two boys and rolled around with them, wrinkling his Brooks Brothers suit.

George didn't say too much to me, but I could see that he was comfortable with me visiting. Some folks you could just tell that they didn't want you to spend a moment longer at their house than you had to.

"Well, you know, Ana likes guests. And you're not a guest, you're family. So I hope you stay long enough so that all the kids get to know their aunt," he said.

I believed him and, oddly enough for me, felt at ease.

Ana had set a dinner table of bowls of gumbo over-flowing with crab and shrimp, and I tell you, I ate and ate until I thought I would burst. Then I saw Ana look-ing at me knowingly, like Yes, we can see why you've gained weight.

Afterward, I tried to stay up to talk, but I was much too beat down to do more than immediately fall asleep on the couch.

Ana woke me after the family had gone to bed and helped me to the guest room.

"Lita, I hope you'll be up to going to the hospital tomorrow."

I stood there rubbing my hair like I had lice, hoping she'd just leave and let me collapse onto the bed, but no, she wanted me to say, "Yes, I will see Daddy with you tomorrow."

Tired as I was, I couldn't bring myself to say that. I didn't want to see Daddy. I didn't ever want to see Daddy.

"Lita?" she asked, again.

I stopped rubbing my hair to look her in the eyes.

"Do you need me to see Daddy with you?"

Ana sighed. I sighed and sat down on the edge of the bed.

"I thought you understood about Daddy. He doesn't have long."

Now, I know if I said the wrong word, that would

ruin everything. Ana would think I was the same bitch that made life so difficult for her. But she needed to know how I felt. Come home, and everybody wants to mourn Daddy like he was a man worthy of tears. How's that going to make me feel?

"You know, Ana, if you want me to go, I'll go, but I haven't spoken to Daddy in all those years because I didn't want to. I never stopped thinking that he was the same bastard that I hit upside the head with a pressure cooker for talking bad about Mother after he beat her into the grave."

"Lita, he's changed."

"How?"

"He's been asking about you. He wants to make things right between you."

I wanted to laugh so bad, I had to hide my mouth behind my hand.

"Right between us? That would be good. I would like to see that."

"Okay, so you'll go?"

"Yeah, I'll go."

Ana gave me another hug and headed out of the room. Finally!

I got down on my knees and said a prayer, that I could get through tomorrow without making things worse between me and my sisters. And I would try not to think of killing Daddy, though I thought about that a lot over the years.

Beat as I was, I still couldn't fall asleep. I twisted about in bed, thinking of my boys and hoping that they were okay. Winston was a good father. I didn't have to worry about that; he'd do fine with them. What kept me up—kept me thinking—was Mother.

Would she come to me? Let me see her, like she had with Ava and Ana? That's why I was here, because I thought she wanted me to be home.

I wondered what it would be like, a real visitation? Not just sensing her, smelling her perfume, but her being there, like how Ana and Ava had seen her. I imagined myself seeing Mother standing at the foot of my bed, in a ghostly light, but smiling at me like she would rarely do in life. She'd take my hands and say that it was okay, that I had done my best for the family. That she loved me and wanted the best for me, wanted me to be happy, and most importantly, she would tell me what happiness is and how I should go about finding some. I had to laugh at the silliness of that. What happiness did Mother know in life other than her love for her kids? Daddy was nothing but a damn torment. Thank God, Mother loved work for work's sake, because she sure did enough of that.

The next morning came quickly; by the time I fell asleep, the sun was rising.

I heard a knock at the door and scrambled out of bed, and there was Ana, holding a cup of coffee for me.

"Lita, I thought we could get to the hospital after breakfast."

"Sure, Ana. I just want a long shower and I'll be ready."

Ana nodded, smiling her relief that I planned on doing this stupid thing of pretending to care about a man I hated. She was my sister, and I had been running from family long enough. I cut myself off, and all it got me was alone. I had to admit that.

I needed to see Daddy, as much for myself as for her.

"Aunt Dot is going to meet us there," Ana said.

I shut the door and sat down on the edge of the bed and drank the coffee black as my mood suddenly turned.

The only thing on Daddy's body of any size was his head. He looked like hell. Skinny as I could have imagined him. His eyes were dark and sunken, but what life there was left in him seemed to reside there. Ana knelt by him and took his skinny hand and muttered a prayer.

I felt embarrassed to see it. She genuinely loved this man.

"Daddy, Lita is here."

"Lita . . ." I heard his voice, weak and wavering. "Lita . . . ," he said again.

"Yes, Daddy?" I managed to ask.

"Come here so I can see you."

I bent down close to him, and he looked me in the eye.

"You put on some pounds."

Ana giggled. I would have giggled too, if it wasn't me getting insulted.

"Come over here," Daddy said, in a strained voice.

I wasn't going down on my knees like Ana, praying to get God on Daddy's side.

"Lita," he said again. I saw Ana looking at me.

"Yeah, Daddy?"

"You look good. Not skinny like before."

"Thanks," I said, dryly.

"I'm glad you came back. I've been holding on, hoping you'd return."

"Yeah, I'm here."

"I know you hate me."

I didn't argue.

"I want you to stay in the house."

"I'm staying with Ana."

"I mean forever. I want you to move in," he said, with conviction. Whatever they had Daddy doped up on must have worn off. Before he looked like he was at death's door, but now he looked like the father I knew, always up to something, looking out for what was good for him, and leaving you holding a bag of shit.

"Isn't Ava living there?"

"Ava moved out. She found a place across the lake," Ana said, saving Daddy the effort.

"Oh, well. But you know I got a house in Los Angeles. My job and kids are there."

"You left that man, that husband of yours. 'Bout time you dumped him. Now, you stay down here."

I heard a door open behind me. I didn't even need to turn my head to know that it was Aunt Dot.

She didn't take a step. I guess she wanted to be able to run out like a madwoman if the impulse struck her. Then I heard her sucking her dentures.

"So, Lita, you back here with us hillbillies. Thought you had forgotten all about us, but I remember you. I remember my favorite niece in the whole wide world."

I didn't know what to say to the woman. I mean, if there were two people that I didn't want to be stuck between, it was these two. I might have hated Daddy more, but he couldn't hurt me, not anymore. Aunt Dot, that malevolent bitch, would put a knife in my back if it meant a dime to her. I didn't want to turn around to face her, worried that I'd be turned to stone or my blood would freeze in my veins—somehow that woman would shorten my life.

"What, you don't have a hug for your auntie?"

Ana giggled again, and even though she'd patched things up with Daddy, she didn't look like she wanted any part of Aunt Dot.

Daddy tried to push himself up onto an elbow. Ana rushed over, glad, I'm sure, to have something to do to keep her from Aunt Dot.

I gave up and met Aunt Dot's eyes.

She didn't look insane like I remembered. No toothy sneer—probably dentures wouldn't allow for that—and her hair, that gray tumbleweed, had been tamed. Now it was chopped short, like a boy's, and though it made her look a little more canine, it was a improvement.

"Ha, you got fat in Los Angeles," she said to me with a happy laugh.

I had to shake my head. Aunt Dot was still able to stick it to me just as easy as ten years ago.

"I guess so. I like your new hairstyle. Bet you miss the spiders and lice you used to have up there."

Aunt Dot smiled at my insult and continued on like I hadn't said a thing.

"So your old man has been talking about the house with you?"

Down to brass tacks. That's what I liked about this woman; it always comes down to money.

"Well, Lita, you know he wants you to live there, but you must know why Ava moved out."

"Now, don't you start with that nonsense," Daddy managed to croak.

"It ain't nonsense. Ask Ana or Ava when you see her. She'll tell you all about it."

"Why don't you just take your crazy stories out of my hospital room," Daddy said.

For the first time I could remember, I was happy with Daddy.

"Oh, shut up, and take this." From her purse she

pulled out a soggy oyster loaf and sat it on the side table.

"You expect him to eat that?"

"Maybe you'll eat it for him," Aunt Dot said, and patted me on the stomach.

Lots of water under the bridge, but not enough to make me forget how she treated me, Mother, and Adele. I managed to catch her hand and dug my nail into her wrist.

She raised an eyebrow and rubbed where I scratched her, drew blood.

"Now, Lita, that was ugly. Guess you feel bitter about the divorce, but I'm sure if you don't get too heavy, you can find somebody else."

I smiled and clenched my fists. I didn't care if we started tangling right there on the floor beside Daddy's bed.

"Lita, calm yourself. I'm not here looking for a fight."

"Good," I said.

"Yeah, you know I'm not the kind of woman who gets down and dirty. I leave that to the monkeys."

"You mean your kids?"

"Yeah, you right. I got some grandkids in the car that'll scratch your face all over again."

My hand shot out with a will of its own and grabbed that disgusting oyster loaf and hurled it at Aunt Dot's head. Caught her flush on the cheek, and just before she could fling the water pitcher at me, the door opened. A nurse entered and wasn't amused to see fried oysters, bread, and what else scattered across the floor.

"What's this? Having a party in here? You need to take this mess outside. This man is seriously ill."

Aunt Dot ignored the nurse and waved to me.

"You, Lita! You got a lot to learn, and I'm going to teach you!"

"Sure, Aunt Dot. Whatever you say."

She shook her head like she was sorry for me, like I needed to be worried. No, I was wrong. I hated that bitch even more than Daddy.

Soon as Aunt Dot was gone, and the nurse swept up the sandwich and left us to act more the fool, I sagged against the wall.

Daddy looked the worse for the visit.

"Well, Daddy, if you ever wondered why I stayed gone—"

He smiled at me, and I returned the smile. I guess nothing brings out love like hate for Aunt Dot. After Ana fluffed up his pillows, Daddy looked ready to fall asleep.

Ana took my arm as we walked out.

"You know that Aunt Dot is crazy," Ana said, like she was telling me something I didn't know.

"I know. Hell, yes! I know she's crazy," I said.

"And she's dangerous."

"Yeah, that's nothing new. You don't forget when someone orders their kids to cut up your face the day before your wedding."

"But she's worse. You've been gone. We all try to avoid her, but she's always around. In everybody's business. Bullying us, trying to get us to do what she wants."

"Don't you worry about that. Last thing I'm gonna put up with is that crazy woman."

Ana squeezed my hand and opened the car door.

"I'm happy my big sister is home."

"And I'm glad to be home, even if I'm going to have to slap sense into Aunt Dot, and you know how hard that's going to be."

8

"*Don't you worry about me, Lita. I don't* mind coming back to pick you up," Ana said.

"You sure you don't want beignet and coffee?"

"Lita, I got to pick the kids up from school, plus, you know, I don't like going places my children wouldn't be welcome."

"That's up to you. I can't see why that should be a problem. They're not here."

"The city's changed. There's a lot of tension right now. You really have to watch your step. Colored people think you're trying to pass and want to knock you on your ass. White people think exactly the same thing and want to knock you on your ass, but then they call the police and get you arrested."

"Nobody gonna arrest me."

Ana shrugged. "Just call me when you're ready. I'll be right down."

I nodded and slipped out of the car when she stopped at the light in front of the Café du Monde. Even though it was a Monday afternoon, the Café du Monde was already crowded with big-bellied, pink-necked tourists.

I found a seat under a fan, near the water fountain. I really wanted those doughnuts because try as much as you like, you can't cook those things outside New Orleans to taste like they make them here. A lady took my order and quickly brought the doughnuts and my café au lait. I ate them greedily, and tried to resist having more.

Really, I hadn't eaten much except for last night's gumbo. That was good gumbo.

I didn't order more beignet, but it was hard work wiping the powdered sugar from my hands and face. I drank my coffee and thought about what Daddy said. I might not like my life out west, but what did New Orleans ever do for me but bring me and the family grief? I'd be a fool. And then there was Aunt Dot. That woman was stone crazy. What the hell was I supposed to do about that? Hit her upside the head with a pressure cooker?

Shit!

I saw Joe come in, looking like he had just run a mile in noonday heat, mopping his forehead with a handkerchief, hair turning gray. His stomach wasn't spilling over his belt, though I half expected it. Specially since he still had the habit of going to the Café du Monde regularly enough that somebody who hadn't been back in ten years could catch him on a first try.

I had wanted to see him, but now I just wanted to slip away and find a phone and call Ana.

I picked up a discarded newspaper off the ground and tried to hide, hoping he'd not notice me.

After a few tense moments I moved the paper aside and saw him sitting a few tables away.

Luckily, his head was down, studying a racing schedule. At least the man was obvious about his vices.

I started to feel silly that I couldn't bring myself to leave, or to call out to him. I was stuck there at the Café du Monde, paralyzed with indecision. "Hey, there, Aunt Lita!"

Startled, I popped out of my chair. I looked up to see this gorgeous boy, maybe eleven, the color of café au lait, and it was like looking into my own face.

"We know each other?" I asked, confused.

"I'm Jean, your nephew. I'm Ava's son," he said, with this wonderful smile.

I had to laugh, and gave him a hug.

"How did you know it was me?"

He smiled, "I could tell. You look like my mother."

What an unexpected compliment, getting compared to my beautiful little sister. I guess in my mind I felt like New Orleans had stopped when I moved away, but life kept rolling along, and now that I was back the city winked, pulling my legs out from under me.

"Auntie, I got to run. They keep us jumping." I slipped him a dollar, and he kissed me on the cheek and rushed off to sit along the chairs where colored kids in white aprons and paper hats waited to sprint to clear tables for the waitresses.

"Lita."

I jerked around to see Joe La Piccolo standing there, smiling at me.

"Hello, Joe," I said. Suddenly bashful, all I could think to do was to fold the day-old newspaper in my hand like it meant something to me.

He pulled up a chair and sat in it backward like big men do.

"After ten years I figured I'd never see you down this way again."

I shook my head. "My Daddy is sick. I had to come."

"Yeah, I heard he wasn't doing well."

I still hadn't met his eyes.

"Lita, well, you ain't changed. Still as pretty as I remember you."

"Thanks," I said.

"How's the family?"

I couldn't bring myself to respond. I couldn't say, "I'm divorced." Instead, I refolded the paper, mumbled something, and ran a hand across my head like I just noticed I had hair.

"You got two boys? Yeah, somebody told me that. Maybe it was your daddy. I got in a card game with him a couple of years ago. He was doing all right back then."

"I got two boys, Winston Jr. and Jude, my youngest."

"How is it out in Los Angeles? You see movie stars everywhere?"

I laughed. "Don't be silly. L.A. is huge. The stars stay far away from people."

"So, you never seen a movie star? Sometimes we get movie stars here. I was working when Jayne Mansfield got her head cut off."

"Really?"

"You should have seen the cops down at the morgue looking at her hooters. It was a zoo."

Suddenly, he looked embarrassed. I didn't care if Joe said something off-color, but the man was actually blushing.

"Sorry, Lita. Sometimes I put my foot in my mouth. You didn't need to hear all that."

"Hear what? Oh, please, Joe. I'm a grown woman. I don't get all red-faced because somebody makes a joke."

"Glad to hear it," he said, looking relieved.

"You have kids?"

Joe looked away and shook his head.

"I had a boy, but he got sick. Ruined the marriage, everything went bad."

"That's awful."

"Yeah, well, that's life."

"Things do get hard."

"Yeah, well, I used to hit the bottle pretty bad. It's what cops do. Kept me from killing myself, but then it got out of hand. Now I just drink sodas and coffee. That made life a whole lot easier. I can get up in the morning, and my head isn't ringing."

"My marriage didn't work out either. Took ten years to realize that we were bad for each other."

Joe smiled, though I could see he was trying not to.

"Life is funny like that. It just sucker-punches you, and then you're supposed to pull yourself together and get on with it," he said.

I glanced at him; that smile of his was gone. Losing a child is the one thing I couldn't stand. I couldn't live with that. Joe choked up, and I felt bad about it.

"Joe, you still go fishing on the lake?"

"Much as I can get out there. I got a motorboat, it's pretty sweet. If you want to go, I'd be happy to take you."

"Sure, Joe. I'm staying at my sister's for the next week or so. Then I'm going back to Los Angeles."

"How about this weekend?"

"Sure."

I gave him Ana's phone number, smiled my good-bye, and hurried out of the Café du Monde like it was on fire.

9

Ana left the kids with George, so it was just the two of us driving out to visit Ava across the lake in Pass Christian. It was a pretty drive, with the water of Lake Ponchartrain on both sides. Spanish moss hanging off cypress and mangrove trees; pelicans perched near fishermen, waiting to steal bait. Ana had a nice radio in her car, and that was good, but she liked listening to country and hillbilly, and that wasn't something I wanted to tap my toe to.

Bored, my mind wandered to Mother again. Why the hell would she appear to Aunt Dot, of all people? She had to be lying, which wasn't so out of character for that cow, but for her, lies weren't enough. She wanted to hurt people, then kick them down and hurt them for real. That was her pleasure, seeing other people suffer.

"Ana, Aunt Dot says that Mother came to her. Did she tell you that?"

Ana shrugged, glanced at me before turning back to the road.

"You know that woman is crazy."

"Yeah, but she said she saw Mother."

Ana turned back to me, and her eyes flashed. "Me and Ava saw Mother. We saw her at the house on Gravier when we were kids."

"Ava told me about that."

"Yeah, that was supposed to be our big secret we took to the grave," Ana said, with a half smile.

"So you don't believe her?"

"Of course not. Mother hated that woman. Why would she waste her time?"

I nodded. I didn't know if I should mention what happened to me, my visitation. I could have been dreaming. Seems like too much of my life is like that, equal parts waking and sleeping nightmares, but at least smelling Mother's perfume wasn't a dream I immediately wanted to escape.

"Lita, what are you so worried about? There's nothing we can do about Daddy but pray. Aunt Dot is a fool we avoid."

"Until Daddy dies. Then you can imagine the kind of shit she'll stir up. I can hear her shouting, 'The house is mine!'"

"You should just try to relax. This should be a vacation for you."

I laughed. I never had a vacation, except for my honeymoon, when we drove to Baton Rouge, if you call that a honeymoon.

"Tell me some more about this Joe La Piccolo."

Now she had me blushing. "What? I'm going fishing with him."

"You never been fishing in your life."

"There's a first time for everything."

"Don't you feel uncomfortable about him being Italian and all?"

"No."

"Not a little bit?"

"What, he's browner than Winston. And I'm not marrying him. I'm not shacking up with him. I'm just going to watch the man fish and eat at some dive he thinks has good food."

"Sounds like a date to me."

"Listen, little sister, I'll tell you all about it soon as I get home."

I put my head back and closed my eyes, but I wasn't tired, I was just tired of talking about Joe. I liked him, always have, but the last thing I needed to do was get hung up about a man.

I didn't tell Ana what I suspected was going on, why Mother might be about bringing me back to New Orleans. I didn't say that it probably had to do with Ava being in trouble and I needed to do something, like I've always been expected to do something.

"What's going on with Ava?" I asked.

"If I had all the hours in a day, I might not be able to explain what your little sister does."

"She's with a new man?"

Ana held up three fingers.

"She's got three men?"

Ana shook her head. No.

"Ava is on her third marriage. And when she's between men, it's just pure crazy. That's why she's out here as it is. Men fighting like dogs wherever she is. I mean, you wouldn't believe some of it. Sure, you know she's pretty, but these guys, they oughta know better."

"They really fight?"

"Oh, God, right out in front of the house on Gravier, with the kids playing outside, two imbeciles showed up at the same time, dropped their candies and flowers and got to drumming and beating on each other until Ava came outside and told them both to go to hell. She made them turn tail and run. All we could do is laugh. She's got some powerful effect on men."

We finally exited the causeway onto the rough roads of Pass Christian. I had forgotten how wild and overgrown that part of Mississippi is. Cicadas whirred away as we slowly made our way to wherever the hell Ava lived.

"So this husband has got to be the charm," I said.

"Yeah, right. She's about to dump him too, but you'll meet him. A nice enough guy, big and strong and looks like he could wring a man's neck looking at him . . .

but you'll see. You have to see this with your own eyes, how your little sister is."

Pretty soon the trees were so tight and dense that the road was canopied by branches. It must have been degrees cooler under that green sky.

Ana kept bouncing along the rutted road, carelessly bottoming out that Cadillac, until the road washed out. Ana backed up a bit and parked in front of a weathered but attractive country cottage with arched gables and fancy shutters. Wild rose hedges grew right up to its windows, and the roof was half covered with blooming morning glory.

"It's pretty, even if it's in the middle of nowhere."

"Ava knows how to pick 'em. She said you can't buy this kind of charm."

"You tried to talk her out of moving here?"

"Yes, I did. It's pretty now, but when she first moved out here, the girl had raccoons like some folk have roaches. You had to shoo them off the porch to get to the door."

"That's not good."

"She likes it in the country," Ana said.

I didn't see any raccoons on the porch, but I did see a shirtless, muscular dark-skinned man on his knees, pounding nails into floorboards.

"Good morning, Johnson."

He looked up, eyes red and teary, sniffling.

"Good morning to you, Ana."

"This is my sister Lita, visiting from Los Angeles."

He stood up, wiped his hands on the back of his pants, and reached out to shake my hand.

"Johnson," he said. "Pleased to meet you."

He knelt back down and returned to nailing.

I glanced at Ana, but she wouldn't meet my eyes. She reached to open the door, but it swung open, and there was Ava.

150

Lord, she was beautiful, in a peach-colored sack of a dress, her hair tied with a red ribbon, a feather duster in one hand and a squirming brown baby in the other. She was gorgeous in her womanhood, with her Spanish eyes, dark curls, long legs, and cleavage women envied, and that had men hammering nails into planks like their life depended upon it.

"Johnson, I told you to stop all that," Ava said. "We talked about this. Come on, now. Get up."

Johnson lifted his head, his red eyes glistening.

"I'm not done here," he said, in a cracking voice.

Ava sighed and led us into the house. She hugged me tightly, like she was sincerely happy to see me.

"I'm glad you came, Lita. We got a lot of catching up to do."

"Yes, we do," I replied.

I don't know what I expected, a bare-walled shanty with kids crying on the floor, spiderwebs in all the corners, and rats' nests just out of sight, but I was wrong. The house was clean and built like a cabinetmaker spent every waking hour trying to make it picture-perfect. The parlor was adorned with oak bookcases and crown moldings, and every door was etched with flowers.

I felt even more envious than I did of Ana's house.

"Johnson is doing a great job. Last time I was here, the walls were bare, and you could see the sun coming through the roof.".

Ava rolled her eyes.

"That's why he can have this house. I'm moving out soon as I get the money. The man works like a maniac. Can't get him to stop pounding, nailing, or sanding."

"That's not a bad thing, if he got talent for working with his hands."

"Oh, he's got talent, but I don't have the patience to live with him."

"What's wrong with Johnson?" Ana asked. "He's got a strong back, a good heart, and he's built like a prizefighter."

"Listen, I don't hold it against him that he did time in Angola. Sometimes a man makes a mistake, and the Lord said we should forgive sinners. I don't have a problem forgiving, but he's hardheaded. He needs to listen to me, but you know, he just keeps pounding nails like that's gonna do the trick and make us happy."

Ava handed me the baby. He smelled good, like he was fresh out of the oven. He looked me in the eyes, smiling just like his big brother did. Just as handsome, but a few shades browner and with big curls just popping up all over his head.

"What's his name? Little Johnson?"

Ava rolled her eyes.

"That's Frederick. Little Freddie. His daddy is in the marines trying to keep as much distance between us as possible, because he knows what I will do if I catch him. Me and Johnson didn't have a baby. Maybe that's the problem. If you don't have a child, it's not a for-real marriage."

152

"Please," Ana said. "In the eyes of most sane people, you married if you have a child or not. I think some states if the marriage isn't consummated, then it's not legal. But I know you two consummated your marriage."

"How you know? Were you a fly on the wall?"

"Come on, the way you disappeared for weeks, dropped your kids off, and honeymooned, right here under the covers."

Ava actually blushed. I never even think of Ava as being the kind of woman who knew how to blush.

"Yes, it was good . . . but that was in the beginning."

"What, you broke his back?"

"Shut up, Ana. What do you know, you little princess?"

"I'm not a princess, I'm a queen. And what's so hard about a man who gives you a house like this, that works as hard as he does for you?"

"Do you know, he can't stand a door to be open. Don't like too many windows open. He spent too much time in jail. Our bedroom is like a cell. He boarded up the windows and got this padlock that he locks us in the room with. I got to fumble with keys every time I got to change the baby."

"What's he afraid of?"

Ava snorted. "You know, at first it was every-thing—people he grew up with, the ones he did wrong, the ones who did him wrong. Guess you get a lot of enemies in prison."

"He's got enemies around here?" I asked.

Ava laughed, and we sat down at the kitchen table, sanded and polished so that you could see your reflec-tion.

"Me. Oh, he thinks I'm out to kill him. Break his heart and take everything from him."

The baby grabbed hold of my hair and yanked, but I barely could feel it. So this is it, what Mother wanted me to do, save Ava from Johnson. Jesus, but look at him, built like he worked the chain gang all by himself.

"Ava, just get your kids and let's go. You can stay with Ana, or at the house on Gravier."

Ava rolled her eyes.

"How's that gonna work? Ana's got enough to worry about without taking me and my three kids in. This place is mine. You think I was serious about giv-ing it away?"

"Aren't you worried about Johnson? He don't look like the kind of man you want to play with."

Both Ana and Ava laughed.

"You worried about me?" Ava asked.

"Well, you mentioned, you know, how Johnson's mad and won't listen to you."

"Lita, that's all true. You were the one who said I can't let a man rule me, and you said a woman has to be ready to shoot somebody to get respect."

"I said that?"

"Something like that. You remember how Daddy made us use that gun in the bar?"

"I remember," I said, "but I never said that you have to shoot somebody."

"You just forgot, or maybe Aunt Odie said it, but you know, I didn't forget it," Ava said with conviction.

"Neither have I," Ana added, and opened her purse and showed me the snub-nosed .38 inside.

"I got the baby, so I can't afford to have the gun lying around," Ava said, and went to the kitchen and reached up into a cabinet and came down with a much smaller gun than the one Ana had.

"This is the one Auntie Odie shot at Daddy with."

"Is this the one? Really?"

"Yeah, she wanted me to have it."

"That's good of her."

Both of them laughed again.

"You should have been there, Lita. Seeing Daddy running and zigzagging, thinking that Aunt Odie had killed him."

"I would have liked to have seen that."

The baby went to sleep on my shoulder, and Ava took him from me.

"I'm gonna put Freddie down. Then I'll start dinner."

I just laughed, soon as she was out of earshot.

"What's so funny?" Ana asked.

"It's crazy. I thought Ava was in some kind of trouble. You know, man trouble. Somebody beating her."

Ana snorted, "Ava lives for a insult. She'll take guff from me or her kids, but not a man. I don't know what happened in Los Angeles, but the little man she brought down here as a husband looked like something the cat drug in. I mean, that boy was her practice toy to get it right."

"Get it right?"

"Oh, yeah. She really knows how to keep a man guessing."

A door opened, and I expected that Ava had returned, but it was a girl, maybe around ten. And let me tell you, she was a princess.

"That's Desiree," Ana whispered.

Desiree sat curled up with a book in the window seat with the wild roses creeping through.

"Desiree, come meet your Aunt Lita."

She barely moved. I wondered if she heard Ana. Finally she turned and smiled. Pretty as her mother, but different. Desiree was lighter than her mother, with long, dark brown hair, without a curl. Three kids in three colors — brown, browner, and white.

"I'm your Aunt Lita," I said.

"Nice to meet you, Aunt Lita," she said, in a voice

that, though girlish, seemed weary, like talking to us wore her out.

"You're not feeling well?"

"I feel okay."

"She's a quiet one. Likes to sit by herself and read. Sometimes she write letters to friends she don't have," Ana said, as if the girl wasn't standing in front of us.

"Nothing wrong with that. I used to read all the time when I had time to hear myself think, but now, if I sit myself down with a book, I'm simply so tired, I just drool and pass out."

Desiree smiled, like maybe she might actually have the tiniest bit of interest in me.

"Where's your brother Jean?"

Her sleepy eyes — hazel, blue? — lit up.

"He's across the lake, working."

"I met him at the Café du Monde."

"He hasn't been home this summer."

She went back to the window seat and her book, looking very sad.

"She's very close to her big brother," Ana whispered to me.

"Oh."

"Her father gave Ava this house. Wasn't much of a gift, until Johnson came along."

"He's white?

"Armand? He's from France, or maybe it's his parents. Somewhere, but I never did figure it out. You know the type, all talk about love and happiness, and soon as Ava married him, he took to staying out all night. Ava straightened that out by shooting up the dining room. Got him to take her seriously enough to divorce her and do right by his child."

"Well, that's good," I said, shaking my head at all the mess I missed out on.

"Desiree, what do you want to be when you grow up?"

"I don't know. I just want to read."

"Read? That's all?"

"I like writing sonnets."

The poor child, she's going to grow up to live alone, in some dark, musty house, waiting for children to come by to give them china-painting lessons.

"Maybe you'll become a teacher. That's a good job."

She shook her head. "No, I don't want to do anything but read."

"But you got to find yourself a job, so you can take care of yourself."

Desiree shrugged. "Maybe somebody will take care of me."

I shut my mouth.

Ana nudged me as we watched the girl in her yellow sundress, willowy and pale, beautiful and fragile, return to her window seat, away from the annoyance of her bothersome aunts.

"Well, that was good, Lita. You got more out of that child than I ever got, and you know she lives with me from time to time."

"Did Ava find her underneath a tree, left by a party of Texans?"

"What the hell are you talking about?"

"Nothing, just reminds me of a story."

"You and your silly stories."

158 *Outside, in the* backyard, we sat on the screen porch, drinking Johnson's homemade peach brandy and eating peanuts. I had the sleeping baby over my shoulder again, listening to his slow breathing against my ear, realizing just what a wonderful sound that is, and half listening to Ava and Ana complain about their men. Good thing about being divorced is that everybody knows how you feel about your man—you can't stand him. I had no interest in complaining about Winston, long ago sick of hearing myself bitch about him. I was surprised when my two sisters turned their attention to me.

"So, Lita, since you been down here, you seem different. You're easy to get along with. Not jumping up to slap somebody down," Ava said.

I shrugged. "I guess you could blame that on Winston—you know, he just made me into an angry, bitchy broad—but that wouldn't be true."

"What's true, Lita?" Ana asked.

"You two think about it. How do you think I felt getting thrown all that responsibility of taking care of you two? I was mad. I stayed mad, and just now, I think I'm getting over being mad."

"So that explains why you were always trying to run us down," Ana said, slurring the words.

"I was just trying to do the right thing, even if I pissed you two off, just like you pissed me off. I was mad at you, and you were mad at me, and that's just how it was."

"Are you mad now?" Ava asked, after taking another sip of Johnson's brandy.

"Depends on whether or not I'm gonna have to change this baby's diaper."

Ava reached over and twirled that baby around and magically changed that baby in two quick heartbeats.

"You ought to see me change a diaper when I ain't been drinking."

Ana laughed. "Ava just rips them diapers off and throws them into the corner, and sometimes she forgets to pick them up until they start stinking to high heaven."

"When I get good and tired of changing them, I just let the baby run around in the backyard naked. It's how nature wanted babies to be, anyway."

"If you want to raise chimps that swing in trees," Ana replied.

All the talk about babies started me to thinking of my own. I hadn't talked to them in a week, and since we were spending the night at Ava's, where there was no phone, it would be one more day.

It was time to think about going home; I was starting to feel guilty about being away so long.

"Ana told me Daddy wants you to stay down here in the house on Gravier."

"Yeah," I said with a shrug. "I can't, but you know I feel different about New Orleans. Before, I couldn't imagine myself living here again, but now I don't know. . . ."

I thought Ava was going to insist that I stay, but she surprised me.

"Lita, you can't stay in that house."

"What house?"

"The house on Gravier."

Suddenly, it was like the temperature had dropped; Ana and Ava seemed frozen with indecision. They were quiet for a time, then Ava spoke. "There's something there. I don't know what it is."

"What?"

"Since Mother died, the house hasn't been right. Even when we were girls the house showed us things and scared the hell out of us, but we knew Mother was there to take care of us, even after she had died. Now it's different."

"What's different?"

"Mother's spirit is angry."

"What the hell does that mean? Mother drove you out of the house?"

"I'm not saying that, but I felt it, how mad she is."

"How did you know?"

"The things she did," Ava said, and shut her mouth and took another swig.

Ana took it up.

"She'd see things, blood on the steps, salted chicken hearts hanging from the back door. Then voices. I heard the voices when we were kids, it's not something you can ignore. It's a racket, Lord, it's loud and you can't escape it."

"So, that could have been somebody else doing that. Maybe Aunt Dot?"

"We thought that too, that Aunt Dot just wanted us out of the house."

"Then Desiree saw Lucien."

I lost my breath.

"Lucien?"

"We're not sure, but she said she saw a man at the screen whispering to her. A handsome man, real handsome, and she kept telling him to go, but he insisted that she open the screen.

"Finally Jean came into the room, and the man ran off," Ava said, "and I went outside to check, and there was blood on the steps."

"Blood? What kind of blood?"

"Lita, do you think I got down on my knees and smelled it?"

"It could have been chicken blood."

"Yeah, and that makes it okay?"

I shook my head. "What do I know, but I still think somebody is trying to get us out of the house."

"But we are out of the house. It's empty, Lita."

"That could change."

Ana leaned forward. Now both twins had their arms wrapped around themselves, and I could see how much they resembled each other, even aside from Ava's cleavage and Ana's red hair.

"Then Aunt Odie showed up and said for her to move out. That there was something wrong, and Ava needed to go."

"Aunt Odie said that?"

I shut my mouth. If Aunt Odie had anything to say about it, then it was the last word.

"Lita, you don't want to know about this. This isn't you. You have a life in Los Angeles. We can handle this. It's our problem."

"I know what you two are saying, but I can't believe it about Mother. She lived her life protecting us. It has to be somebody behind this."

"Lita, it's hard to believe this if you haven't seen it with your own eyes," Ava said, speaking slowly and carefully.

I shrugged and took a deep drink of the peach brandy, then threw down the glass and danced about the porch, trying to get a goddamned flying cockroach out of my hair.

10

A few more days of reacquainting myself with the family and New Orleans, and I'd be ready to head home. I had been a good girl and did my bit to make Daddy believe we had reconciled enough for him to meet his maker with some hope, however thin, that he wouldn't spend eternity burning.

I felt good about myself; this trip that I hadn't wanted to make had gone better than I could have ever imagined.

For the longest time, my relationship with my sisters had been so messed up that it didn't seem possible for it to improve. But ten years was long enough to scrub away the bitterness and the resentment on both our sides. I had been heavy-handed and even cruel to them, but I didn't know any other way, plus my temper wasn't a help. I thought they did their best to try to take advantage of me, just like Mother took advantage of me. We needed to be as far away from each other as possible for the smoke to clear. The bad feeling had to run its course.

Good things do happen.

I didn't expect it, but my sisters loved me, and I loved them.

Unexpected is an understatement.

My only regret is that I hadn't seen my cousin Richie, but Ana and Ava didn't have a clue how to contact him.

Only one thing worried me now before the godawful bus ride back home: fishing with Joe. It would be my last Saturday in New Orleans, and Joe had already left two messages to remind me about the date. How could I forget? My stomach churned, thinking about it.

He said he'd show up early Saturday for us to head out to Lake Ponchartrain. He meant early, too. The sun wasn't up when a groggy Ana showed up at my door.

"Lita, your man is here."

"He's not my man, he's a friend."

"Whatever you want to call him is okay by me."

"Go back to bed, and don't be a cow."

She muttered something and left me alone. I looked

at myself in the mirror. My jeans fit good, and my blouse, this pastel thing, made me look almost as shapely as Ava, I hoped.

I walked to the door, nervous, worried that this date would be awful, but it was too late to back out now. Resigned to my fate, I flung the door open.

There he was, tall and handsome, with a silly fishing vest covered in odd lures and whatnots and a straw hat so ratty that it was unraveling in most places.

"Morning! We'll be the first boat out."

"Great!" I said.

I looked to the driveway and saw a patrol car.

"They let you use these cars on the weekend?"

"Sure! If you don't get caught."

He opened the door for me and handed me a thermos.

"Be careful, it's hot. I got coffee in there, and I made sandwiches too."

I nodded, but I didn't think I'd have too much of an appetite. My stomach still didn't like this idea of a date.

"You know, since I got me this little place in the Quarter, I don't really need a car. I walk to work. I hardly ever leave the Quarter, since it's my beat, and I don't like to be anywhere else. Now that I'm not drinking, I get up pretty early, and it's funny as hell to see all these red-eyed idiots wandering around trying to find their cars. Yeah, to think I was one of them red-eyed idiots not too long ago."

I had to smile. Joe was damn proud to be off the

hooch. Must be tough, though. Drinking hard in New Orleans is like going to church; everybody does it.

The drive to the lake and the docks was short. The boat was bigger than I expected, with comfortable seats and a place to sit your drink. He ran about the boat, working hard to get us underway, and soon we were far out in the lake.

"Now, Lita, once the sun gets overhead, it's gonna get boiling. You might feel silly wearing this, but it'll keep you cool."

He unfolded this huge, floppy sun hat. I'm sure I looked like a fool, but he wanted me to try it on.

He laughed when I did.

"That'll work."

Then he busied himself getting fishing poles ready for us.

"What are we trying to catch?"

"I'm not picky. I'll eat just about anything in this muddy pond."

Soon enough the sun started to beat down. I was happy to have the hat, but I still felt like a lobster slowly boiling to death.

Joe didn't seem to even notice. He caught fish after fish. Grinning with satisfaction, he tossed them on ice and kept on fishing. Finally I caught something, a funny-looking croaker that Joe pulled off the hook and cut up for bait. It wasn't the blood and guts that made me queasy, it was when he stabbed the fish; it croaked, then moaned, low and long, until Joe finished killing it.

I did not care for that, no damn talking fish. We would still be out there, frying in the sun, but Joe turned around and saw a black dot on the horizon.

"Damn," he said, and pulled the fishing pole out of the water. "Look at that squall coming our way."

The dot grew bigger, but still looked like nothing to be worried about. But Joe revved up the boat, and we raced back to shore anyway. Not a minute too soon. The black dot now covered half the sky, and a stinging rain already pelted us. Waves churned up out of nowhere, rocking the boat like a toy, and winds roared in all at once. You couldn't see the shore just a hundred yards off.

"Lita, hold on. We're almost to the docks," he said, one hand steering, the other holding on to that ridiculous hat.

I don't know how Joe could have seen the dock, but he did. We bumped hard against it, and I don't think I ever was so happy to bump into anything.

He struggled to secure the boat, then struggled to get me up the ladder onto the pier. The rain was so heavy, I could barely open my eyes.

We ran, stumbling, to the patrol car.

"You wet?" he asked after we were inside. The rain drummed relentlessly against the roof of the car.

"Now that's a stupid thing to ask."

Joe shrugged and wiped his wet face with a sopping wet handkerchief.

"We could have drowned," I said, thinking about it now that we were back on land.

"Yeah. I've been fishing my whole life, and I never been in a squall that bad."

"See, I'm bad luck," I said.

"Sugar, the only luck I've ever had is bad, so there you go."

Soon the clouds parted, and you could see the sun glaring down and the steam rising from the ground.

"I should get you home," he said, looking at me like the last thing he wanted was to get me home.

He leaned toward me, and we kissed. It was nice, though he tasted like coffee, lots of coffee.

*W*hen *he got* back to Ana's, we kissed again. Again, it was like stale coffee, but I was getting used to it. If he drinks coffee the way he used to drink beer, he must have been a hell of a drunk. As much as the kissing was fun, we weren't kids, so I felt uncomfortable hugging up in a police car in the middle of the day. That's like saying to the world, Take a look, I'm making a fool of myself.

After the third kiss, we said good-bye. I walked to the house, feeling embarrassed to be in my skin, sure that I was being spied on.

Ava opened the door before I knocked, crying and exclaiming. I felt mortified, sure she was upset at me.

She wrapped me in her arms and laid her head on my shoulder, sobbing uncontrollably.

She couldn't get it out, but I knew. Daddy had died.

"It's okay. He's gone, but he'll always be with us," I said. "Do you want me to make phone calls?"

"Sure, Lita . . . I made out . . . a list of family . . . who need to be . . . called."

I did my best to shed a tear, tremble, and sigh, for Ana's sake.

I led her back to the house, called George so he could come home to comfort her, and called the relatives. They were surprised and taken aback to hear my voice, thinking, maybe, that I had died back in Los Angeles. I called the church to arrange the funeral service, called the mortuary, called to see what kind of food we'd have.

Ana sat, her head on the kitchen table, crying.

I rubbed her shoulders and got a wet rag for her face. She was inconsolable. I convinced her to go back to bed, worried a little that she might fall out of the chair and crack her skull with all the crying. I took a shower and tried to figure out a way that I could miss the funeral. I figured that since everyone would notice my dry eyes and the look of anger that would pass over my face as Daddy's moral uprightness was remembered, the best thing would be for me to stay away.

The doorbell rang, and through the window I could see Aunt Dot.

Ana called from the bedroom for me to get it.

Walking across the carpet, I dragged my feet, hoping that if nothing else, she'd get a shock.

I opened the door, and there she was, smiling like a dog about ready to stick its nose into some shit.

"Hello, Aunt Dot. What brings you here?"

"What did you do to get him to leave the house to you?" she said, contempt overflowing her words.

"What?"

"Don't act like you some kind of imbecile. I know about your daddy's will. That house belongs to me as much as anybody. Who the hell are you to come down here and claim it?"

"I'm sorry to hear that," I said, and shut the door.

She rang the bell again.

"That was my father's house, and I have as much right to it as anybody! I want what's mine!" she said through the door.

"Listen, Aunt Dot, don't make me lose my temper. I don't know a damn thing about what's going on. So leave me the hell alone."

"Don't think it's gonna be settled like this. I have as much right to that property as any of you. I got kids, they deserve something from their grandfather too. All of us are gonna sit down and work this out, or I'll swear to God, nobody is ever gonna live here. You understand me! I'm not gonna take your shit, just like I didn't take Helen's shit."

"Don't you mention my mother's name."

"What, you think your mother is some kind of saint? I whipped her ass, and I'll whip yours too!"

Sometimes you take mess because you have no

choice. You just have to put up with it. But I couldn't think of one thing keeping me from slapping the hell out of Aunt Dot.

So I did it.

I hit her so hard that she fell to her knees.

"Don't you threaten me!"

Aunt Dot struggled to get to her feet, and I stood there ready to knock her down again.

George pulled up just then and saw me with my hands on my hips and Aunt Dot looking like she was ready to kill, and me waiting for her to give it a try.

I'm sure George had to be wondering what kind of family he had married into. A college-educated man, he did the smart thing; he stepped back and called out to us, hoping that we would come to our senses and not beat each other's brains out right there on his steps.

"You bitch!" Aunt Dot shouted, lunging for my face with her fingernails.

I slapped her again, and George shouted for us to break it up and dropped his briefcase, not a good thing to do with Aunt Dot around. She'd probably slip away from the fight just to steal it. George shoved us apart before more damage could be done.

"I'm gonna hurt you good," Aunt Dot said, before yanking her arm from George and storming away.

"What was that all about?" George asked.

I smiled and tied my hair into a bun before answering him.

"Sometimes you've got to slap some sense into Aunt Dot."

George looked lost for words.

"I apologize for this, George. Things got out of hand."

"I'm sure you had your reasons. Aunt Dot can be a bitter pill to swallow, but there must be a better way of resolving these things than a fistfight."

I had to smile at him. Ana had married well.

"If you have any ideas of how to handle Aunt Dot that don't involve slapping her down, please let me know," I said, and left the man to go pack my things.

"*I need to* get out of your hair, Ana, and since I got to stay those extra days, it's best for everybody that I stay there."

"Oh, Lita, I like having you here."

"I like being here, but your husband isn't too happy seeing your sister and aunt trying to kill each other in front of his house. Poor man has every right to send me packing as it is."

"George isn't like that."

I shrugged and didn't say anything, but he had been avoiding me ever since the big blowup.

"See, until I came back he probably thought he married into a typical family, you know, with typical kinds of fights, but now he sees just how crazy we are."

"You think we're crazy?"

"Crazy? Oh, yeah, by most definitions, but you know that."

Ana shook her head.

"Nothing to worry about. Craziness skips a genera-tion. It's our grandkids we'll have to worry about."

"I'm going to go lay down," Ana said, and walked away looking worried and exhausted.

That worked well. Now she was ready for me to move into the house on Gravier as much as I needed to go.

11

The house on Gravier wasn't the same. Most of what I knew as a girl was gone, lost in the fire, gutted and torn out. All the detail—the oak floors, the cabinets, leaded-glass windows, glass doorknobs, fancy light fixtures—all of that replaced on the cheap from the local hardware shop. Maybe that's why Ava took up with Johnson, so he could make for her the kind of house we were raised in.

Sad to walk through and see each room missing all of what was memory for me. Most of the furniture was gone except for the bed in Mother's room. I guess Ava slept there when she lived in the house, but that would be the last place I'd sleep. Now I didn't have a choice, unless I wanted to sleep on the floor. The old stove was still there, just how it was when I saw Daddy come at Mother trying to drown her under the faucet, the same night I cut Daddy and he knew better than to ever touch Mother again if he didn't want to die. By the window, below the sink, I could still make out where the hole was repaired in the floor where Lucien hacked his way inside, trying to get at Mother and the girls. Mother threw the pot of boiling water on him and sent him screaming back down. You think he would have learned then not to mess with us, but he kept coming. Through the kitchen I stood in front of the door that led to the bar, the bar that made my childhood so hard.

It was locked. I rattled the door, kicked it, thought about trying to find something to break it down, then I just got tired.

I wondered if I should really spend the night here. The electricity wasn't on, and wouldn't be until tomorrow. The gas wasn't turned off, so I could take a bath and wash dishes, and that was good. I really didn't want to leave; it felt good to be home for the first time in a long time, and it made me want to stay and crawl into bed and never leave.

The house was so dusty and the air smelled so stale that I opened every window. Ana had given me bedding and a pillow, and it made sense to make the bed, give me something to do until Joe came by to take me to dinner.

If only there was somewhere else in the house to sleep, a couch, but I guess I could sleep on the floor. I put Ana's lantern by the door, and near to it candles and matches, to be ready for the night, and next to that I put a claw hammer to be ready for Aunt Dot.

Lately I hadn't slept well, so after making the bed, I stretched out on it and shut my eyes for a minute.

Saw myself alone in a house that should, that needed to, be filled with family. A house that witnessed so much—Mother giving birth to us, raising us, and grieving for us, and her dying, all happening here. All of it, our sad story entwined in the walls.

I closed my eyes and slipped away.

Awake or sleeping, I don't know, but I heard something—crying? A child crying. The house was dark, and I bolted from the bed. Smelled smoke, heard that crying again; it wasn't a child, it was me.

I crossed the floor to open the door; the handle burned, sizzling my palm.

The unbearable heat of the room dropped me to my hands and knees. I crawled backward away from the door, then realized I had to get out of the bedroom, and that was the only way. I reached up to grab the handle, turned it through the pain and opened the door, crawled into the hallway, heard voices, shouts, Mother's voice and a man's voice.

Smoke and fire, a reddish black that illuminated nothing. A figure came through—Mother, weak and bloodied, her arms cut, slashed, stumbling into the fire. Then another figure, a big boy dragging Mother from the house. A pounding, pounding drumming, and the house exploded. Drumming, drumming, more drums, my name shouted over and over again over the drums. Weeping, I wanted to stand and run, but the heat forced me back to my knees. Blind and alone, air burning my nose, my throat.

"Lita, Lita!"

Pounding, exploding all around.

Light, coming toward me. White, not red, clear light. See, to see. See him there, a man, and I screamed.

Pounding, pounding, I pounded his chest. Light fell up.

I saw him.

"Lita, it's Richie. Wake up!

I woke, crying in a dark house, to a cousin who came for me.

*O*n *the porch* I shivered, freezing though it was another hot New Orleans night. Richie sat on the last step, sipping from a beer, staring down the street like he was looking for someone or something.

"How did you know I was here?"

Richie spat between his feet.

"I didn't know. I just keep an eye on the house, keep bums away. Sometimes I sleep here."

"I had a crazy nightmare. Never had one like that. I was on fire, the house was on fire. I saw Mother, all messed up, and you dragging her out of the house."

Richie shook his head.

"I don't want to talk about that. It ain't right to talk about what happened."

"Do you ever see her—Mother?"

Richie was always a big kid. Now he was a big man. He had a gut, but was well built otherwise. Heard he was a fisherman, and he looked like one.

"I don't talk about her. If you say those kinds of things, you make people think you're crazy."

"I saw her. I'm not crazy."

"People always think I'm crazy. I don't talk to them. I don't like people. I don't have many people to talk to. Sometimes I see her when I'm here. But I don't talk to her. I just see her, like you saw her, like in a dream. You feel her."

"Feel her? What do you feel when you feel her?"

"Sad. I feel sad for her, like she's alone, lost, and can't find us."

Richie stood up.

"I'm gonna go fish. But you better lock them doors and windows. My mama might be coming by here. She's got you on her list."

"I know."

Richie pulled a bike out of the weeds, along with his fishing pole.

"Richie, you going to be back around here?"

"Nope, not tonight. My girl lives down by the river."

I watched him ride away, and I sat there on the

steps of the crazy house I was supposed to spend the night in, and I knew I wasn't going to sleep one minute.

I felt like an idiot. I barely could stand Richie and didn't treat him like I should have, and he comes in and drags me out of a nightmare.

But it wasn't just a nightmare, it was real.

Jesus, how could Ava have lived here?

I crept through the door, found the lantern, and turned it on. Nothing but an empty room, and no one there with a straight razor ready to cut me up.

Lucien was dead, and Mother was dead, but her spirit was here and grieving.

Aunt Odie.

She'd know.

With the candles and lantern I had enough light to feel comfortable about stretching out on the bed.

Then I thought about Aunt Dot, and I got out of bed and checked every door and window to make sure the house was locked up tight.

Where the hell was Joe?

To hell with him. I got out of bed and headed outside to sit on the porch with a cup of tepid water to cool me on a hot night that would be too long if it lasted an hour.

I don't know how long I had fallen asleep for, but when I heard Joe's "Hey you!" I must have been out for a while.

"I know it's hot and all, but I don't think you sleeping out on the porch is a good idea."

I sat up, stretched, and shook my head.

"I didn't mean to fall asleep. I kind of took a nap."

Joe shrugged.

"Sorry I'm late, but there's a sweep going on in the Quarter. Rousting the pros and towing everything else in sight. Lot of overtime, but they just keep us working."

"That's okay," I said.

"Lights off?"

"Yeah, but I got candles."

"Tell you what. I'll take you back to the Quarter, and we can get something to eat. Then I should be able to get off, maybe we can find you a hotel."

"I'm fine here. Don't you worry about me."

He laughed. "Okay, Lita, whatever you say."

"Let's go," I said. "I'm hungry."

The Quarter is worse than a madhouse on a Saturday night. Joe parked the police car in front of a Italian market, right in the red, blocking traffic, and got out to open the door for me. Cars jockeyed to get around us, but that didn't seem to bother Joe. Without a look back, we went inside. At the counter Joe ordered po'boys for us. The cashier had a huge stomach hanging over his pants and a big gun holstered to his waist that you almost couldn't see if you were looking straight on at him.

"Thanks, Googie," Joe said, and turned around and went back for cold drinks.

He didn't pay a cent. I guess that's how the police make it, getting their little lagniappe.

As we were about to get into the car, Joe turned to me with a nervous look on his face.

"Lita, if anybody asks you, just say your purse got stolen, and we're driving around looking for it."

"Sure," I said, surprised that anything at all bothered this man.

"My sergeant might be walking his dumb ass around looking to bust somebody's chops."

I shrugged and he drove us to the Café du Monde and again left his car in the street, and we sat by the fountain and ate our sandwiches.

"How you holding up, you know, with your daddy passing?"

I shrugged and didn't say anything. Instead I watched the crowd, flowing by us on their way somewhere. Yeah, it was a Mardi Gras without Lent.

Then I saw some colored kids running as fast as they could, laughing and carrying on, shoving people, just acting the fool.

"Hey, you little sons of bitches! Get the hell out of here!" Joe said, and leaped up and started after them.

It was so sudden that I took a couple of steps after Joe. He grabbed one kid and yanked him backward and kicked him in the butt.

"Back the other way, asshole."

Another boy appeared alongside me.

"Hey, you white bitch!" he said, and spat in my face.

I swung my purse at his head but missed, and Joe tore off after him.

I hurried to the rest room and washed my face. I looked at myself in the mirror and saw that white lady he spat on, and sighed. New Orleans was like that, a city that jumps up and spits in your face for being white even when you're not.

I returned outside, sat at a table far from the street, and waited for Joe to return. I had two doughnuts before he got back. I saw him before he saw me, craning his neck, checking the tables, his blue shirt stained with red splotches.

He hurried over when he saw me.

"What was that about?"

Joe snorted. "That's been happening lately. Colored kids who knew better than to come to the Quarter to start trouble are now showing up and causing it," he said with bitterness. "Now, we got to crack heads, and you know, there's other stuff, militants causing real problems. Cops getting shot at in the projects. Hell, I wouldn't go to Desire at night. No f'ing way."

"Then you got these crackers showing up with bats wanting to start trouble with the coloreds, and we're in the middle of that. Everything's changing all at once, and I don't know what's gonna happen."

I was quiet for a minute, then I had to remind him.

"Joe, I might not look like those boys you were chasing, but that's who I am."

Joe looked me in the eyes.

"Lita, I know who you are. My family's been here a long time. We were treated like we were colored. My grandfather got lynched by a mob looking for Italians who shot a cop."

I sighed, and thought about how crazy this all was. Getting spat on for being white. Seeing a white man who thought of himself as much of a colored as I was. Or at least he said that.

"You go to work. I'm going to sit here and eat doughnuts until the sun comes up," I said.

Joe nodded. "I'll be back soon. I'm about off."

"Sure," I said. Soon as he was gone, I found a taxi and headed off to Ana's.

12

The *funeral* *mass* *for* *Daddy* *was* *at* *St.*
Catherine's, the same church I was married in so long
ago.

Daddy had friends, lots of friends, to see him go to
his heavenly reward. I wonder if they've got penny
slots in Heaven. Most pews were filled with his old
buddies, men on their last legs, looking pickled and
confused, as if church was something they did only at
Christmas, or when they had a pint or two to keep the
anguish down. I kept overhearing "Doc this," or "Doc
that," and for the life of me I couldn't figure out why
anyone would call Daddy "Doc." Doctor of what?
Maybe he was doctor of the con, of running the serious
scam. That was my father, a bloodless operator.

The funeral was about as bad as I thought it would

be, with family all up front, so we could view the coffin
and hear the priest and shed the tears and make it into
a real scene. My sisters did their part, and even Aunt
Dot, sitting not that far from us, with her brood of
appropriately grief-stricken demon children and grand-
children. Not me, though. As I expected, I sat dry-
eyed, like at Mother's funeral. Then I was too angry,
too bitter, to cry, but on the inside I was a mess, so
grief-stricken that if I gave in to despair just a little I
would have been hopeless, sobbing on the floor on the
church like a madwoman. This was different. I couldn't
fake it, what I didn't feel, and I didn't feel anything.

The service ended quickly and mercifully for me. It
did get embarrassing, though, when Daddy's friends
started a chant of "God bless, Doc," as we were filing
out to the cemetery.

Then, before we left the pew, Aunt Dot had to act
the fool. You could hear her coming forth with howls of
manufactured grief, reverberating around the church.
Did she think we were going to pay for her hysterics?
Then her kids joined in—yeah, she'd be demanding
money for services rendered—sobbing and carrying on
like Daddy was their daddy. Well, their daddy was a
drunk. He ran away soon as he got the message that if
he didn't, Aunt Dot would kill him, so maybe that's not
a good comparison. Anyway, with all that going on,
nobody paid attention to me. All I needed to do was
stay close to Ava, and nobody would glance in my
direction. Hard to imagine the black dress she wore

could fit any better or tighter. She looked wonderful, red-eyed and wet-cheeked. The priest spent too much time consoling Ava, too. He got the attention of Johnson, who afterward put himself between the priest and his wife like he was her rock of ages.

Then, as we were milling about outside the church, George came up with a stunned Ana.

"What's wrong?"

"Tell her, George," Ana said, and turned away.

"Gloria is here."

Ana pointed to an unhappy woman in a awful-looking wig.

"Who's Gloria?"

"Your father's second wife."

"Yeah, so? He divorced her a long time ago."

George shrugged. "She claims to have a will to the house on Gravier."

Ana, cool, calm, educated Ana, turned red.

"You know, I'm of half a mind to pull that cow's wig off and beat her ass up and down the street."

George now looked stunned, as though those words couldn't have come from his wife's mouth.

"Ana, we are not making a scene in public. We don't need to be seen acting like animals fighting in the street."

Then he glared at me, like I was the ringleader who turned his wife into a street-brawling wild woman.

Ava came over to see what was going on. Ana managed to convey it in so few words that it had to be some kind of twin talk.

"What, that bitch!" Ava was even more enraged than Ana. "Do you know how she treated us when we were girls?" she said, shouting at me like I was going to defend Gloria.

George took Ana's arm and tried to lead her away, but she yanked free.

"Go see about the kids, I'm talking to my sisters."

George looked shocked, then angry enough to have it out with Ana right there on the street. He must have noticed how we locked ranks around our sister, how grim-faced, and goddamn mad we were. That was it, he was beat. George wandered into the crowd to find his children for the drive to the cemetery.

"What are we going to do?" I asked.

"It's not real. I'm sure the heifer faked it," Ana said.

"Yeah, but it could slow things down," I replied.

Then Ava started toward Gloria, and Ana pulled her back.

"We can't do that. I think George might just have a heart attack."

It came to me; looking over, I could see Aunt Dot and her brood staring at us, like hyenas waiting for wildebeest to stray, and I knew what to do.

"Ava, are you on speaking terms with that lunatic?"

"Speaking terms with what lunatic?"

I nodded to Aunt Dot.

"Oh, yeah. I'm on her good side."

"What side is that?"

"Her backside."

"Listen, go tell her that Gloria has a will to the house. That'll take care of it."

"Lita, that's a mean and vicious thing to do. I mean, I try to live a life that Jesus would approve of, and though that woman is a backbiting snake who tried to take advantage of two girls who just lost their mother, and who once tried to turn their daddy against them, I can't just toss her to the lions."

Now I had heard everything.

"Ava gets like this sometimes," Ana said with disgust. She took a few steps toward Aunt Dot, then waved to her, probably realizing that she didn't want to get too close.

They exchanged a few words. Aunt Dot smiled, like it wasn't anything serious. Then Ana pointed out Gloria. Aunt Dot nodded and turned to her children. The big boy in front looked to be at the most fifteen, and an assortment of children of various ages followed Aunt Dot over to Gloria.

Gloria looked around and realized she was surrounded, but still she stood her ground. Whatever people say about her, she was a brave woman. Our hearse came up, while I watched with morbid interest as Gloria shook her head. She refused to hand over the will, like any one person could stand up to that, an angry Aunt Dot with her clan behind her, an Aunt Dot who thought that somebody was trying to cheat her out of money. The circle closed around Gloria on the steps of the church, and as we drove off to the cemetery, I swear I saw a wig tossed into the air.

Ava sighed and sat back, holding the hand of her daughter, Desiree.

"You shouldn't have had to see that."

"Should we go back and help her?" I asked, just for the hell of it.

"What, are you crazy? That woman doesn't deserve anything more from us than pity, and very little of that," Ava replied.

*S*ince *it was* hot and threatening to rain buckets, the priest got through the "ashes to ashes, dust to dust" quick, and we were done. Ana was having the family gathering at her house, and she took me back to the house on Gravier so I could get a change of clothes.

I just needed a minute in the house to grab my things. I hurried to the porch, concerned with how difficult it would be to settle Daddy's estate. Would it even be worth the bother? Then I saw it, staining the front porch. The sight took my breath away. Must have been a bucket's worth of blood. Blood on a hot day.

Plump flies swarmed about, intoxicated with it. My disgust multiplied: guts were wrapped about the door handle like some macabre ribbon.

I backed up, thanking God it was daylight.

I walked back to the car, and Ana hurried out to meet me.

"You look like you saw a ghost."

"See!" I said, pointing to the porch, to the blood. Ana didn't get as close as I did, but she was even more alarmed than me.

"Let's go."

190

We hurried into her car, but then a crow, the biggest crow I had ever seen, landed on the porch, looking about like it expected company. The damned bird was right. As we sat there in that hot car, sweating, paralyzed with fascination, more crows settled in on the porch.

Ana put the car in reverse and roared out of there.

"Lita, our family is cursed. It's got to be cursed. Things like this don't happen to ordinary families."

I shrugged.

I had no idea of what to say about that. All I knew was that I was stuck in a hot black dress for the rest of the day.

*N**either one of* us said a word on the ride to Ana's. I didn't even know what I was supposed to think about what I just saw. It was supposed to scare me, that much I knew, and I was scared.

Had to be Aunt Dot.

She wanted us to sell the house so she'd get her share, though she wasn't entitled to anything. I guess if you didn't want to have guts all over your door, you better consider whatever she had to say.

Couldn't say it scared me any more, though, than seeing Mother in that dream.

You expected a certain amount of craziness from that Aunt Dot, but not Mother. I just thought Mother would be happy in the next life, doing whatever people do there. But it wasn't like that. It was a mess. I had to get to the bottom of this before I went home. I didn't care about the house, about the money for selling it, about any of that. I wanted to know why Mother wasn't at rest.

I looked at Ana, but she answered me before I asked.

"Of course it's Aunt Dot. She must have stopped by on her way to St. Catherine's and had one of her brats toss the blood onto the porch and thrown around those pig guts."

"Yeah, I'm sure you're right."

"Don't say a word to George. After everyone is gone, we'll go back and clean up. I don't know, Lita, but I'll be glad when we're done with that house. It's just a big headache."

I nodded, but I didn't think this big headache was going to be settled easily.

*A*na's *house* was filled with hungry mourners who, in lieu of a second line and strong booze, made like pigs, chowing down on the elaborate spread. Ana had wanted me to hire waiters, and they did look impressive in starched white shirts and black pants and jackets, going about with trays of ham croquettes and meatballs.

"I don't know why you think you needed servers. It's damn expensive," I said to her, between greeting guests.

"You only have one father. I wanted to show respect."

I nodded.

"Plus with George and his position, we have to have a dignified gathering."

"Well, I guess he didn't see what happened to Gloria."

"No, he didn't. And he doesn't need to hear about it, either."

Just then, we heard a commotion at the door. Coming into the foyer were Aunt Dot with just a small complement of her usual entourage of kids. The big boy was there—I think his name was Bobby, or Kerby— but I intended to stay as far away from him as possible, so I hoped it didn't matter that I didn't know.

A waiter was brave enough to try to stand between the boys and the dining table, probably because they were stuffing food into their mouths and pockets like something out of Dickens, but they shoved him aside like a storm surge does a dike.

Ana interceded and quickly shooed the boys away

with threats to tell their mother. Then she found Aunt Dot grimly rummaging through the refrigerator. They seemed to share a friendly conversation, and soon after, Aunt Dot and her brood left.

"What was that about?" I asked when she returned.

Ana's eyes glinted.

"Oh, I asked how did the thing with Gloria go, and she showed me Gloria's will."

"Well, that solves that," I said, feeling good about getting something out of Aunt Dot's wolf pack other than getting my face scratched up.

"And she said she made the boys return her wig. Probably because she didn't know what she would do with a wig like that but scare folks."

"That's kind, for Aunt Dot. She's softening in her old age," Ana said.

I stepped outside to see for Ava. But there was Aunt Odie coming up the walk, as usual all in white; though it was a hot day, not a bead of sweat was on her forehead.

"Aunt Odie, this is a surprise! Last thing I thought was I'd see you at Daddy's funeral."

Her face was hard as stone, barely registering my greeting.

"I need to talk to you two and Ana."

I nodded, as did Ava.

"I'll try to find her."

"Now, Lita."

"She's got guests."

"Tell her to leave them. We've got things to discuss."

I shrugged and headed into the house. Ana stood next to her husband, looking into his eyes as he talked to a Negro man in a very nice suit. It had to be somebody important. George's eyes darkened, but he grudgingly introduced me.

194

"Lita, this is Professor Bledsoe. He teaches business at Xavier."

"Pleased to meet you," I said, and shook his hand.

"And what do you do, Lita?"

I batted my eyelashes and lied.

"I plan to go back to school soon, I think to get a degree in business."

George rolled his eyes when I patted Professor Bledsoe on the shoulder.

"Maybe I'll get to be one of your students."

Professor Bledsoe looked very happy with that idea, but I was through flirting and pissing off George. I took Ana's hand and led her outside, where Aunt Odie waited for us.

Ana looked as surprised as I was to see Aunt in the shade of a willow tree on the edge of the property.

"Aunt Odie, I'm glad you could come."

"I'm not here for this. I'm here to tell you about what you sisters need to do."

Ava came over, and the three of us stood there facing Aunt Odie, waiting for her to take us to school.

"Okay," I said, "what's going on?"

"You three need to stop running away. It's your mother, Helen, and she needs you."

Ava and Ana looked as confused as I did.

"You all need to go there, all three of you."

"Aunt Odie, I don't know about that. I had a nightmare there. It just scared me, scared me bad," I said.

Aunt Odie's hand darted up and slapped my face.

"Listen to yourself. She needs you. She's calling out to you, and you three ignore her. If you loved her when she was alive, if you love her now, you need to go there."

Ava's face turned red.

"I love Mother as much as anybody, but I'm never going back to that house."

Aunt Odie slapped Ava just as suddenly as she had slapped me.

"You have to go back to the house. You have unfinished business, all three of you."

Rubbing her face, Ava squinted at Aunt Odie.

"You don't know what I saw there. What she did. My babies couldn't sleep. Johnson won't even let me mention her name around him. I thought Mother loved me, but all I felt was rage."

"Rage?" Aunt Odie said. "Maybe she has a good reason to feel rage."

Then Aunt Odie looked at Ana, as though she expected her to say something that would get her slapped too.

"What about you?" Aunt Odie asked, looking at Ana.

"I don't know anything about this but what they told me. I don't have those dreams or anything like that."

Aunt Odie slapped her. Ana rubbed her cheek, looking relieved to get it out of the way.

"That's because you never would go over there. You stayed far enough away that you couldn't, wouldn't hear," Aunt Odie said, putting her finger into Ana's face.

"Hear what? What is it she wants us to hear?"

Aunt Odie shook her head. "That's not for me to tell you."

"I'm willing . . ." I said.

Ana said, in a low voice, "I'll go."

Ava's jaw tensed. She didn't look happy about this conversation. "You two can do whatever you want, but I'm not going back to that house."

"She needs all of her children there," Aunt Odie said with finality.

"Why don't you go?" Ava remarked, and she was the first of us to get slapped twice.

"I'm not her daughter. She didn't love me more than she loved her own life."

"Will you come with us?" I asked.

Aunt Odie's cold anger lessened.

"I'm ninety-two, and I'm not going to be in this world very much longer. It's just a short walk from here to there. Going to that house might just start me on my way."

I heard her words, but I wasn't paying attention.

She was right about Mother. I wanted this, to feel Mother again in my life, but it had scared me. What I had felt scared me now, but still, I had to go back and see it to the end.

"Ava has to go?" I asked.

"Yes."

Ava refused to meet our eyes and returned to the porch, where her daughter and husband waited.

"We'll go; I'm betting she'll follow."

"But Lita, did you tell Aunt Odie about the blood?"

I shook my head, remembering.

"Someone tossed pig blood and guts all over the porch."

"I did that," Aunt Odie said, as matter-of-fact as though she had left flowers and candy.

"Why?"

"Your aunt Dot would have left more surprises for you. She is capable of almost anything."

"But blood and guts?"

"Oh, she would have left plenty worse things. It's disgusting, but to her, someone who has a heart as black as hers, she knows, it's a warning to her. To torment your mother, she'll go very far, and I needed to leave her a message that she wouldn't go unchallenged."

"What do you mean?"

"Aunt Dot possesses a malevolent spirit. Where she goes, evil follows. She doesn't need to summon the Orishas. Dark spirits flock around her like hungry vultures, waiting for her to leave them a carcass. Bad as your father was, as selfish and cruel, he's not in the league of your aunt Dot. When Adele ran from Lucien, she stayed with me in the country for a while. He came for her when I was asleep and took her back. There was no one who knew she was with me but your mother. No one knew where I lived, but you girls and Aunt Dot. Never put anything past Aunt Dot. She did almost anything to hurt Helen, helping Lucien to take Adele from her in this life, and taking the house on Gravier from her in the next."

We held each other, on that muggy evening, crying for our dead mother, who still grieved for her children.

13

I was as happy to see bugs circling around the porch light when we arrived—the electricity was back on—as I was to see a man sitting on the top step, smoking a cigarette.

It was Richie. I hurried out of the car.

"Richie, watch out for the blood."

Richie stood up, stretched, and tossed down his cigarette.

"I cleaned it up. Took care of the guts, too."

Now, even in the dim, yellowish rays of the porch light, I could see the blood was gone.

Ana still sat in the car, looking frightened. I opened the car door and gestured for her to come out. She started to cry.

"Ana, it's okay, we're here together," I said.

She wouldn't look at me, but she clasped my hand and held it so tight it hurt.

At the porch, Richie stepped aside and lit another cigarette.

"Thanks, Richie. I didn't want to clean up that mess."

Richie took another drag of his cigarette and nodded.

Ana wouldn't look at Richie and kept me between them.

The screen door was unlocked and the front door was open. I took a step inside, and the house seemed empty, quiet, and settled.

"Come on in, Ana."

Ana followed like she did when she was a toddler, grasping my hand and craning her head to see what was up ahead.

I waved for Richie to join us, but he wouldn't.

"I don't go in uninvited."

"I'm inviting you."

"Sorry, Lita, but you're not the one who's got to invite me."

I let that go and didn't bother to ask him to explain himself.

"You want a cold drink or something?"

"Naw, I'm okay outside, plus I got a job to do."

"What's that?" I asked.

"I'm waiting for my mother."

"Waiting for your mother?"

"Yeah, I'm supposed to keep her out of the house and out of your hair."

"Who told you to do that?"

"Auntie Helen."

"Oh," I said.

Ana had disappeared inside. With the lights on, the house didn't at all seem as scary as my first night.

I found Ana at the locked door of the bar, with her head leaned against it, crying.

"What's wrong?" I asked.

"Being here after so long," she said, after a long sigh. "God, the things we've gone through."

"That's true."

"This isn't so bad with Richie out there, watching the house for us."

"Yes," she said, but still she cried. I wasn't too surprised. Memories flowing in like the tide can overwhelm you. Still, though, seeing her cry made me panicky.

"Richie should go," she said.

"There's hardly any furniture but the bed in Mother's room. If you want to lie down—"

Ana refused to meet my eyes.

"Richie should go."

Ana looked exhausted.

"Come on," I said.

I had managed to make Mother's room look like somebody lived in the house. I had made the bed and swept the floor, got things looking lived in, but Ana sat on the edge of the bed, tears streaming down her cheeks.

"I don't know what this is supposed to accomplish," she said.

"I don't either, but Aunt Odie knows what she's talking about."

"But without Ava, it doesn't even make sense for us to be here, just like Richie."

"Look, Richie might not be a Du Champ, but he's a cousin. He's more than that—he's been like a brother to us."

"Lita, Richie just disappeared. Some say he drowned."

I shook my head like she had been doing since we got here.

"He doesn't look drowned to me."

Ana tried to explain between pauses to wipe the tears from her face.

"We didn't talk to you about it because it just seemed too much, with Daddy and everything else."

"What?"

"Richie's been gone for a long time. We heard he had been working a boat in the Gulf. Then we heard he was lost. Now, here he is."

"It must have been a mistake."

Then we heard a shout.

We both ran to the door. Aunt Dot was there, and Richie was running around throwing his hands up, as if he was trying to ward off a swarm of bees. His eyes were as big as saucers as he frantically dashed about. Finally he disappeared down the street.

"That boy is too stupid to stand up to me."

Then Aunt Dot seemed to pull herself together, and she approached the porch again. I noticed the small leather bag she had around her wrist, and wondered what she planned to do with it.

"Did Helen think that would do it? Scare me off? No, I'm here for what's mine. And you two can't stop me."

She opened the pouch and pinched between her fingers something that looked like sand. She tossed it at us, and it burned my eyes.

"What the hell is wrong with you," I shouted, "throwing salt in my face!"

She pushed me aside and headed into the house and didn't stop until she was at the door to the bar.

Ana stood paralyzed as I followed, determined to drag Aunt Dot out by the scruff of her neck, but the supposedly locked door swung open, and she escaped into the bar.

I took a deep breath and followed. I expected the worst—fires roaring around me, ghostly knife fights, screams of mortal terror—but it was just the bar, dilapidated, and cobweb-covered, smelling of wood rot and rat droppings. But I blinked, and the room looked like how I remembered long ago when Mother saw to it, spick-and-span clean. There were sounds of folks partying, smoke hung in the air, the jukebox was playing, and men were crowded against the bar, waiting for drinks. Behind the bar stood Lucien, serving a beer to Aunt Dot.

"Mrs. Du Champ, it's good to see you again."

I gasped and turned to leave, but his voice, that voice rich like shit-stained honey, had me stuck there, a bug in amber.

"See, Lita, this house is mine. Why would you want to live here anyway? Because Helen wants you to? That bitch is gone, and I'm the one who drove her out."

I heard a pounding on the door, and Ana's voice calling for me.

My sister hadn't deserted me!

"Lucien had as much blood spilled here as anybody. He had as much grief with Helen as anybody, and you've got to give the devil his due."

Then Lucien came toward me, the Lucien that was a young man, a handsome man, a man so handsome that your knees weakened when he smiled at you. He reached for me, reached his arms around me, and crushed me against his chest.

His mouth found mine, and I could taste river water, I could feel that box around me as it sank lower into the cold depths of the river, felt the breath forced out of my body as I inhaled the Mississippi.

Then I heard Ava's voice along with Ana's, shouting for me to open the door, the sound of crashing, then I felt the trunk lift, pulled upward, dragged onto land, the trunk lid being ripped open, and me, gasping air, as my sisters pulled me free.

We were by the front door, Ana and Ava kneeling next to me, wiping the stinging sweat from my face.

Then we heard the door open like we did when we were young and Mother came home from the fish market, heard her heavy footsteps coming toward us. I caught a glimpse of the straps of her favorite heels as she passed, and looked at the hem of her yellow pleated skirt as she continued on through the parlor into the dining room, through the kitchen and on into the bar.

I tried to struggle to my feet, tried to run after Mother, desperate to help her face Lucien and Aunt Dot, but I barely could stand.

"We need to get to the bar."

"No, Lita, I'm not going near there," Ava said.

"Then stay!" I said, and struggled to my feet and teetered on.

"Wait, Lita!" I heard Ava shout. Both she and Ana came up, and together we returned to the bar.

We heard the sounds of struggle on the other side of the door. Ava and Ana hung back, but I flung the door open.

The bar was what it was, a deserted shell that verged on collapsing in on itself. The only difference was that the boarded-up back door had been ripped open, and we could see Aunt Dot struggling with a man, our Richie.

We followed them outside. Richie did his best to

shove Aunt Dot back as she struggled to get around him.

"Go home, Mama! Aunt Helen don't want you here."

"Get out of my way, you goddamn turncoat."

Aunt Dot tried to slip by one more time, but Richie, striving mightily, held off that hellcat.

"You're not getting back in. It's over."

With the three of us blocking the door and Richie doing the dirty work, Aunt Dot gave up and turned to leave.

"You owe me, Lita. If you think you gonna live here, you got another thing coming."

Then Aunt Dot fell to her knees, like she had been belted by a invisible fist.

That did it. Aunt Dot looked about for who might have hit her, but none of us was within striking distance. That seemed to unnerve her, because she looked about and then took off almost at a run.

With his big arms wrapped around himself, Richie watched Aunt Dot disappear into the night.

"Y'all should go in. Auntie got something to say to you before she got to go."

The three of us returned to the house, hand in hand. Mother was there, cleaning the zinc counter, looking radiantly happy. She looked up at us with such love in her eyes.

And I shared that feeling of happiness, the contentment of being home with family after a grueling journey.

"All I ever wanted was for my girls to be happy, for our home to be a home, and you, Lita, to realize I loved you as much as I depended on you, and I depended on you with the weight of the world. Nobody could take that dream from me, I'd never be that far away."

Mother put the polishing rag down and straightened her back. She picked up her purse and made her way to the door. There Richie met her, and she handed him a peculiar-looking wooden box, waved good-bye, stepped outside, and vanished.

I didn't bother to follow her. I knew she was gone, but it was about daybreak, and I wanted to see that, the sunrise.

*W*hen *I told* Joe what we wanted to do, he didn't seem to mind, but I knew he thought it was strange.

Early the next morning, we crowded into his boat, and he piloted us out to the middle of the river. Richie seemed to have a good idea of where he wanted to go. For a ghost, he seemed to eat a lot of tuna sandwiches and drink lots of soda pop.

"I just didn't have nobody I wanted to tell I got home okay," he said about his ship sinking.

Richie never had a lot of spare words, and about Mother and all that he had very few, but where we were getting to on the river he had a lot to say about.

Richie told Joe to stop and then opened a bag and

pulled out a wooden box and a hammer. He drove a nail into the lid, cursing Lucien under his breath.

He handed the box to me. It felt like it was filled with lead. "Lucien Furie" was scrawled in Mother's handwriting across it. I drove a nail into it, as did Ava and Ana, and we all cursed him and his mother and the horse he rode in on, and most importantly, his memory.

Then Richie took the box and hurled it into the dark waters of the Mississippi.

You'd think a box filled with lead or rocks or whatever Richie had in there would sink like a stone, but it didn't. For a moment it seemed to struggle to stay afloat, bobbing about, but finally it sank.

I prayed that no storm would ever vomit up that box back onto shore, but Lucien was some vile. Maybe not even the Mississippi has an appetite for him.

14

Joe sat on the steps of the house on Gravier, with flowers in hand, refusing to come in until I took off my apron.

"I'll put them in water. Come on in and join us," I said.

I grabbed his hand and yanked him up. Everybody was in the small kitchen, taking a break.

Thanks to Johnson, the bar was back to looking like it used to, even better, with new stools and floors, and Johnson had finished tarring the roof.

Jude stood in the corner of the kitchen, looking out of the window. He had yet to get used to New Orleans or being away from his older brother or his daddy, but that couldn't be helped. New Orleans was his home now, as it was mine.

Joe turned to me after inspecting the progress on the bar.

"It looks good, Lita. Guess you'll be a bar owner soon enough."

I smiled and put my head on his shoulder after I was sure Jude wasn't looking.

"I guess it's in my blood, serving liquor to bums."

"I'm fine with it, as long as you got fresh coffee for me."

I pointed to the coffee urn that I had just purchased.

"For you," I said, and he blushed. Odd man, blushing because his girl buys him a coffeepot.

Desiree walked into the kitchen, her head buried in another book, looking like some kind of sprite in a white dress and her hair done up in ribbons and plaits.

Jude turned to see her, and that melancholy that had plagued him since he came to New Orleans vanished from his face. He followed Desiree as she blindly wove her way through the crowded kitchen out into the backyard.

After finding a vase for Joe's flowers, I fixed him a sandwich and put him to work hanging drywall. I returned to the kitchen, looked through the window, and saw Jude and Desiree underneath the big magnolia tree, talking like they had known each other for all their lives. What next? Jude asking me if it was okay to marry his cousin, Desiree? I could see myself in the near future, telling him under no circumstance was that a possibility, but for now, if he was a quarter as happy as I was, I wouldn't mind him having a crush on his cousin. We'd have that bridge and many more to cross soon enough, but not today.